M000215914

tHe Lees of LauGHteR's END

the Lees of Laughter's end

a tale of

BAUCHELAIN & KORBAL BROACH

BY STEVEN ERIKSON

NIGHT SHADE BOOKS
SAN FRANCISCO

First Edition

ISBN

978-1-59780-144-7 (Trade Hardcover)

978-1-59780-145-4 (Limited Edition)

Night Shade Books
http://www.nightshadebooks.com

WEST OF THEFT, THE TITHE STRAIT OPENS OUT INTO the Wastes. A vast stretch of ocean through which naught but the adventurous and the foolhardy dared brave the treacherous, dubious sea-lanes as far as the Red Road of Laughter's End, and from there, onward to the islands of the Seguleh and the southern coast of Genabackis, where the lands of Lamatath offered sordid refuge for pirates, wastrels, the rare trader and the ubiquitous pilgrim ships of the Fallen God.

What launched the free-ship *Suncurl* out from the sheltered waters of Korel and Theft was a matter known only to Captain Sater and, might be, her First Mate, Ably Druther. Such currents of curiosity, as might lead one to speculate on said matters, could reach out and grasp a soul fierce as a riptide, so Bena's mother warned in her whispering, rattling way, and Bena was not one to clap ears in stubborn

1

countenance to such stern advice.

Not while her mother remained with her, to be certain, never silent for long with that wave-rolling and wind-sighing voice, the 'waring whistles, wry hoots and mocking moans as true and as familiar as any music of the heart. Why, her hoary hair danced in the wind still, reaching out to brush Bena's young, smooth and—it was said well below—tantalizing features as Bena crouched in her usual perch in the crow's nest, her maiden's eyes thinned as she studied the western Wastes with its white-furled waves and not another sail in sight, waiting as was her mordant responsibility to first spy the darkening of the waters, the grim blood-dark seas that marked Laughter's End.

A full week out now from Lamentable Moll's cramped little harbour, and at night Bena listened to the hands below muttering their growing fears, decrying the endless creak of the nails in the berths and bulkheads, the strange voices rising from the hold and from behind the strongroom's solid oak door—when all knew that there was naught behind it but the captain's own gear and the crew's stowage of rum, with the captain alone holding the fang-toothed key to the enormous iron lock. And in answer to all these goings on, with surety blood had been let over the side in the darkest bell every night since, each hand spilling into the cup their precious three drops from a stippled thumb.

Had some curse clambered aboard in Lamentable Moll? Mael knew, there was nothing good arriving in the guise of the passengers they had taken on there. A highborn toff with a spiked beard and cold, empty eyes. A rarely seen eunuch, the highborn's companion, and as their manservant none other than Mancy the Luckless, who—she had learned—had swum from more wrecks than the Storm Riders themselves, or so it sounded. *Fare begone these wretched guests,* Bena's mother muttered again and again whenever *Suncurl* pulled a peg or two to correct course, and Bena would huddle down as the mast tucked and tilted, heaved and dipped, tipping the wicker basket of the crow's nest hard over so that she could look up and, on occasion, see the bend of waves.

Wayward as the wind 'ere, beloved daughter, them guests, and see yon again that crow, oh fluttering black wing in our wake, why, nary a strip of bleached coral for fifty leagues since the Shingles yet the be-demon spawn bobs and slides dark as a regret! Look yee that crow, darling, and make no nest 'ere for one as that!

Oh, Bena had not heard her mother moan so in all the time that they'd shared this nest, and so, with a gentle caress, Bena reached out a hand to stroke her mother's wispy hair, only a few strands coming away from the parched, salted scalp above the shrunken, sightless eye sockets.

Huddle me come for company this night, darling daughter, for ahead soon runs the blood-dark seas of Laughter's End, when the nails shall speak their dread words. Hold ever, sweet child, to our tiny home here high above—we'll suck down the last snot of those gull eggs and pray for rain to slack our throats and lo, you will cry in delight to see me swell into ripeness once more, my darling.

Huddle me come for company this night!

And now, far to the west, Bena saw as her mother had said she would see. The vein of blood. Laughter's End. She tilted back her head and loosed a piercing cry to announce to those below the long-awaited sighting. Then added a second cry, *Bless the begging, if you would, send up another bucket of vittles and the rum ration, please yee, before night is birthed! And,* she added to herself, *yee all die.*

⌒ ⌒ ⌒

As the wordless animal cry from Bena Younger in the crow's nest faded, First Mate Ably Druther clambered up onto the aft deck and stood beside his captain. "Only a day late for the blood-dark," he said, "and given this buffeting wind that's been pushing us round, that's not too bad."

Hands on the wheel, Captain Sater said nothing.

After a moment, Ably continued, "Them dhenrabi are still in our wake. Expect they're heading for the Red Road just like us." When he still received no reply or comment, he edged closer and in a low voice asked, "Think they're still after us?"

Her expression tightened. "Ably Druther, ask that again and I'll cut your tongue from your mouth."

He flinched, then tugged at his beard. "Apologies, Captain. It's a bit of the nerves, y'see—"

"Be quiet."

"Yes sir."

He stood at her side in what he hoped and came to believe was companionable silence, until he was comfortable enough to decide that some other subject was acceptable. "Sooner we get Mancy off this ship, the better. Ill luck squats in that man's lap, according to the hands we brought on in Lamentable Moll. Why, even back on the Mare Lanes I heard tales of—"

"Give me your knife," Captain Sater ordered.

"Captain?"

"I don't want your blood on mine."

"Sorry, Captain! I figured—"

"You figured, yes, and that is the problem. It's always the problem, in fact."

"But this thing 'bout Mancy—"

"Is irrelevant and stupid besides. I'd order the crew to stop talking about it, if that'd work. Better to sew all their mouths shut and be done with it." Her tone dropped dangerously. "We know nothing about the Mare Lanes, Ably. Never been there. It was bad enough you blabbering in Lamentable Moll that we'd hailed from Stratem, which was as good as pissing on a tree-stump for the ones on our trail. Now, listen to me, Ably. Carefully, because I will not repeat this. For all we know, they've hired themselves a fleet of Mare raiders, meaning we've got a lot worse tracking our wake than a few dozen bull dhenrabi looking to mate. Just one word that the Mare might be looking for us is enough to start a mutiny. I hear anything like that from you again and I will cut your throat where you stand. Can I be any clearer?"

"No, Captain. As clear as can be. We ain't never been to the Mare Lanes—"

"Correct."

"Only the three who came with us keep talking about them lanes and our run through 'em."

"No. They don't. I know them well. Better than you. They're not saying a word, so if the knowledge is out, it's because of you."

Ably Druther was now sweating in earnest, and tugging frantically at his beard. "I might've made mention, once. But careless then and I ain't careless no more, Captain, I swear it."

"Careless once and the rest don't matter."

"Sorry, Captain. Maybe I can make it seem like I'm a liar. You know, lotsa tall tales and the like, exaggerations and worse. Why, I know one story—from Swamp Thick, that nobody'll believe!"

"They might not," she replied slowly, "except everything you've ever heard about Swamp Thick happens to be true. I should know, since I was bodyguard to the Factor there for a time. No, Ably, never mind trying the liar's route—your problem is not just that you talk too much, it's that you're stupid besides. In fact, it's a damned wonder you're still alive, especially since my three friends have had to listen to you night after night. Even if I don't murder you, they probably will, and that could make things complicated, since I'd have to execute one or all of my oldest companions, for killing an officer. So, all things considered, I should probably demote you right now."

"Please, Captain, talk to them! Tell them I won't say another thing ever again, about anything! By Mael's own spit, I swear it, Captain!"

"Ably Druther, if you weren't the only one of us who actually knows which end of a ship points where we're going, you'd be long gone. Now, get out of my sight."

"Aye, sir!"

ᔕ ᔕ ᔕ

"Cook's a poet," said Birds Mottle as she sat down opposite her friend.

Heck Urse nodded amiably, but said nothing as he was stuffing his mouth with food. Few others around in the galley, which was how Heck, Birds and Gust Hubb preferred it. Gust had yet to arrive, which left the two of them and only one other and that one was on his own bench, staring down at his bowl of grub as if trying to read in the jumbled mash his future or something. Which wasn't a thing a man like Mancy the Luckless should be doing, as far as Heck was concerned.

But never mind him. They'd been months now on this damned stolen ship, and while things had been a little rough at the start, it had settled out some—all the way until the harbour of Lamentable Moll. But now, Heck had come to realize, things were getting rough all over again. Mancy the Luckless was the least of their worries. The damned ship was haunted. No other possible explanation. Haunted. As bad as the Catacombs of Toll's City, voices and wraiths and whisps and creaks and crackles and shuffles—no, wasn't rats neither, since no-one could recall seeing a rat since Moll. And when rats jumped off a ship, well, that was bad as things could get, or nearly almost, by Heck's reckoning.

Rough at the start, aye, for Sater and the three of them here now no different from any other salts. But none of them were. Salts, that is. Not Sater, whose captaincy had been in Toll's City palace guard—before the Night of Chants, anyway. And not Heck, nor Birds nor Gust, all of whom had been sentries at the city's southeast corner gate that fateful night. The fifth in their motley group, Ably Druther, they'd picked up at Toll's Landing, but only because he knew stuff about sailing and he'd had the runner they'd needed to cut loose of the Stratem mainland. And he was handy enough with that cutlass so that stealing the *Suncurl* had proved a whole lot easier than it probably should have been.

Ably Druther. Just the name made Heck scowl over his empty bowl. "Liabilities," he muttered.

And Birds Mottle nodded. "Captain's own word, aye. And this is where we are, Heck, sure as the clock-lock chunks on. Wonder," she added, "if those dhenrabi are hungry."

But Heck shook his head. "Word is they don't eat during mating season, which is why all those sharks are staying close instead of whirling away so fast they break the waves like they was trying to fly. The males will fight once we're well along the Red Road, and the sharks will get fat. So I'm told."

Birds Mottle scratched at her short hair and squinted with her bad eye, which was what she did when struck by some unpleasant thought. "I ain't never hated the sea more than I do now. It's like we're trapped here, as good as in any prison, and day after day the view don't change one bit. And with all the creepy sounds we're hearing…" She shivered, then made the Chanter Sign with her left hand. "It's no wonder we're all having nightmares."

Heck leaned forward. "Birds, best keep that signing to yourself."

"Oh. Sorry."

"Chances are," Heck said by way of mollification, since he loved Birds with all his heart, "nobody here has heard of the Chanters. But best be safe anyway, since we don't none of us want to be… liabilities."

"You got that right, Heck."

"Besides, I found us a good answer to those damned nightmares. I got us switched over to night watch."

"You did?" That bad eye squinted even tighter.

"What's wrong?" Heck asked. "Don't it make more sense—after all, sleeping during the day and the nightmares won't be nearly so bad, right?"

"I'd wager the ones you traded with are dancing

on the boom right now, Heck. You shoulda come to me first, so I could put some reason in your head. Night watch, Heck, means maybe coming face to face with what's scaring the runnels outa us."

Heck Urse paled, then made the Chanter Sign. "Gods below! Maybe I can switch it back—"

Birds snorted.

Sagging, Heck stared down at his bowl.

At that moment the third Stratem deserter, Gust Hubb, bolted into the narrow galley, his eyes wild and so wide the whites were showing on all sides. One hand was clamped over one ear and there was blood running down that hand. His pale fly-away hair waved about like a frenzied aura. He stared at Heck and Birds for a moment, his mouth working, until words came out: *"When I was sleeping! Someone cut off my ear!"*

⤚ ⤚ ⤚

SEATED A SHORT DISTANCE AWAY, EMANCIPOR REESE, Mancy the Luckless, was jolted from his contemplation of myriad peculiarities by the sailor's panicked entrance. Sure enough, once one of the others managed to get Gust to pull his hand away, the ear was missing. Deftly sliced clean off leaving a trickling streak of red and peeled-back skin, and how the man had slept through that was a true mystery.

Likely drunk on tipped-in illegal spirits and the victim of some feud in the crew's berths, Emancipor concluded, returning his attention to the bowl of food before him. *"Cook's a poet,"* one of the swabs had said, before wolfing the stuff down. Madness. He had sailed plenty of ships and had weathered the fare of a legion of cooks, and this was by far the worst he had ever tasted. Indeed, it was virtually inedible, and would be in truth if not for the copious amounts of durhang he had taken to stuffing into his pipe along with the usual rustleaf. Durhang had a way of making one ravenous, sufficient to overcome the dreadful misflavours of such malodorous staples. Saving that, Emancipor would now be nothing but scrawn and bone, as his wife Subly was wont to say whenever any of their spawn came down with worms and some pronouncement was required—although she was wont to say it with a tinge of envy in her tone, given her girth. *"Scrawn and bone, by the blessed mounds!"*

He might even be missing her right now. Even the urchins of questionable seed. But such emotions seemed as distant and left behind as the harbour of Lamentable Moll. Less than a hazy smear on the horizon, aye, and let's have another bowl of durhang.

Listening in on the conversation of the swabs—

before the arrival of their one-eared companion un-leashed a flurry of shock, concern and then nervous speculation—had left Emancipor the vague sense that something was indeed awry with those three. Never mind the adamant opinions of the rest of the crew that these sailors knew a ship like a mole knows a treetop, and that maybe Captain Sater knew even less, and if not for the First Mate they'd have all long ago run aground or into some dhenrabi's giant maw. No, there was even more to it, and if only Emancipor could pull the thick webs from his thoughts, why, he might have an idea or two.

Eager hunger beckoned, however, slowly trans-forming this bowl of consumptive goat spume into a delectable culinary treasure, and before long he too was cramming the horrid stuff down his throat.

The bowl rocked and he leaned back, startled to find his meal suddenly done. And here he was, lick-ing his fingers, pushing the ends of his moustache down into his mouth to suck loose whatever gobs had clung there, then probing past his lower lip with a still urgent tongue. He looked around, furtively, to see who might have witnessed this frantic, beastly be-haviour, but the three swabs had left—rather quickly, he recalled, to seek out the ship's medic. Emancipor was alone.

Sighing, he rose from the bench, collected the

wooden bowl and, dropping it into the saltwater cask near the hatch, made his way onto the mid-deck.

A bucket of food was being hoisted up to the crow's nest atop the mainmast, and Emancipor looked up, squinting in the glare. They all said she was pretty, the daughter, that is. But maybe mute— hence the eerie cries wafting down every now and then. And as for Bena Elder, why, a squall witch, she was, and had not come down, not even showed her prune face since before Moll—and life was better for it, aye. Well, strain as he might, he couldn't see anyone up there.

Still, a nice thought to think the young one was pretty.

Smiling, he made his way aft. It was good to smile these days, wasn't it. Belly pleasantly full and mostly quiescent. Fair sky overhead and a decent wind caressing easy swells on the sea. Subly far away and the imps with worms crawling out of every orifice just as far away, as, well, as Subly herself. Murdered employers and crazed killers and—oh, right, some of that, alas, was not so far away as any sane man might prefer.

Worthy reminder, aye. He found himself standing braced to the roll and pitch near the aft rail, pushing rustleaf in his pipe bowl, his blurry vision struggling to focus on the black-shrouded figure hunched against the stern rail. On the fat, pale fingers working with precision on the hook and the weighted line. On the round, pallid face, a sharp red tongue tip visible jutting up over the flabby upper lip, and those lank, low-lidded eyes, the lids and lashes fluttering in the breeze.

Focusing, aye.

As Korbal Broach worked the severed ear onto the barbed iron hook.

Then flung it over the side and began letting out loops of line.

⌇ ⌇ ⌇

THE NAILS CREAKED WITH THE COMING OF NIGHT, AND those creaks were the language of the dead. There had been much to discuss, plans to foment, ambitions to explore, but now, at last, the voices grew in urgency and excitement. Trapped in the nails for so long now, but release was coming.

The Red Road that was Laughter's End beckoned, and wave by wave, the thunder of cloven swells rumbling along the timbers of the hull, wave by wave, they drew yet closer to the grim vein, the currents of Mael's very own blood.

The Elder God of the Sea bled, as was the way of all things Elder. And where there was blood, there was power.

As night opened its mouth and darkness yawned, the iron nails bound to the ship *Suncurl*, nails that had once resided in the wood of sarcophagi in the barrows of Lamentable Moll, began a most eager, a most hungry chorus.

Even the dead, it is said, can sing songs of freedom.

⌒ ⌒ ⌒

"IF YOU WOULD, EMANCIPOR REESE, EXTRACT MY CHAIN armour. Scour, stain and oil. If I recall, no repairs are necessary beyond these simple ablutions, and given your present condition, this is fortuitous indeed."

Emancipor stood just inside the cabin door, blinking at his master.

Bauchelain's regard remained steady. "You may now heave yourself into motion, Mister Reese."

"Uh, of course, Master. Armour, you said. Why, I can do that."

"Very good."

Emancipor rubbed at the back of his neck. "Korbal Broach is fishing."

"Is he now? Well, as I understand, he has acquired a sudden need for shark cartilage."

"Why, do his knees hurt?"

"Excuse me?"

"Squall witches swear by it, sir."

"Ah. I believe, in Korbal Broach's case, he has in mind some experimental applications."

"Oh."

"Mister Reese."

"Master?"

"My armour—no, wait a moment." Bauchelain rose from where he sat on the edge of his bed. "I believe we have arrived at something of a crisis in our relationship, Mister Reese."

"Sir? You're firing me?"

"I trust it need not come to that," the tall, pale-skinned man said, adjusting his brocaded cloak, then reaching up to stroke his pointy beard. "This voyage has, alas, seen a marked degradation in your skills, Mister Reese. It is common knowledge that excessive use of durhang had the effect of diminished capacities, of chronic ennui, and the obliteration of all ambition in the user. Your brain, in short, has begun to atrophy. You proceed in your waking period through an unmitigated state of numb stupidity; whilst your sleeping periods are occasioned by an inability to achieve the deeper levels of sleep neces-sary for rest and rejuvenation. This has, alas, made you both useless and boring."

"Yes sir."

"Accordingly, for your own good and—more importantly—mine, I am forced to confiscate your supply of durhang for the duration of this voyage and, if necessary, from now on."

"Oh, sir, that would be bad."

A single eyebrow arched. "Bad, Mister Reese?"

"Yes, Master. Bad. It's my nerves, you see. My nerves. They aren't what they used to be."

"And what is it, Mister Reese, that so assails your nerves?"

Well now, that was the question, wasn't it. The one all the durhang was letting Emancipor avoid, and now here was his master demanding a most sordid level of sobriety, in which all escape was denied him. Suddenly mute, Emancipor pointed at a massive wooden trunk set against one wall.

Bauchelain frowned. "Korbal Broach's child? Why, Mister Reese, this is silly. Has it ever escaped? Indeed, have you not seen it but once, and that at the very beginning of this voyage? Furthermore, have you no faith in the bindings and wards I have set upon that modest homunculus? Paranoia, I should add here, is a common affliction among durhang abusers."

"Master, every night, I can hear it. Burbling, moaning, gurgling."

"Proper mouths and vocal tracts do not rate much

importance in Korbal's estimation. Such noises are entirely natural given the creature's physical constraints. Besides," and all at once Bauchelain's tone hardened, "we will ever have guests in our company, many of them far less pleasant that my companion's quaint assemblage of organs and body parts as now resides in that chest. I was under the assumption, Mister Reese, that you accepted this commission in fullest understanding of such matters. After all, my principal hobby is the conjuring of demons. While my companion, Korbal Broach, explores the mysteries of life and death and all that lies in between. Is it not a given that we will all experience a plethora of peculiarities during the course of our adventures? Indeed, would you have it any other way?"

To that, Emancipor Reese found no possible reply. He stared, gaping, his eyes locked with that of Bauchelain's.

Until the sorcerer turned away, with the faintest of sighs. "In any case, Mister Reese, the child should not be the source of your disquiet. I believe I spoke of this matter with you before—shortly upon our standing down for the open seas, in fact. This ship was in Moll Harbour for both re-supply and repairs, in addition to taking on new crew. Of these purposes, it is the repairs that are relevant to our impending situation."

Pausing, Bauchelain walked to the stern port and

leaned both hands on the frame as he bent to peer through the lead glass. "Ah, dusk approaches, Mister Reese. And in moments we shall be in the throes of Laughter's End. Iron nails, Mister Reese. Purchased in Lamentable Moll."

Emancipor frowned. Now, mention of that stirred something in his head. The voices of two friends in a bar. Kreege and Dully, aye, the scroungers. *Nails. Iron nails….*

Bauchelain glanced back at Emancipor. "Tell me, Mister Reese. Since you are a native of Lamentable Moll. What, precisely, is a *Jhorligg?*"

◝ ◝ ◝

HECK URSE KNEW HE SHOULD BE SLEEPING, RIGHT UP UNTIL the bell sounded the night watch, but his mind was a maelstrom of anxieties, terrors and niggling worries. It was understandable, wasn't it, that the shift over of duties from day to night would require some awkward adjustments, a stuttering transition, aye. And while Birds Mottle seemed able to plunge into deep slumber at a moment's beckoning, well, she'd been in the auxiliary of the Crimson Guard garrison at Toll's City, hadn't she? Close to a real soldier as any of them. As for Gust Hubb, truly the man's luck was impressive. Imagine, losing an ear just like that, and there was the ship's cutter pushing into his hands a bottle of D'bayang nectar and a mouthful of that you could sleep through Burn's own bowel movement no matter how many mountains fell over.

Alas, poor Heck Urse still had both ears, and none of a soldier's talent for sleeping anytime anywhere. So here he stumped about, restless and wobbly as a whiskerless cat. And there at the stern rail dead ahead was one of the guests, the fatter one that nobody ever saw except when they did and that wasn't common at all, except there he was, all cloaked in black and the hood drawn up.

Heck thought to wheel about, but then he'd be passing right by the captain again and once without a comment or command was lucky enough but twice was damned unlikely. Instead, and with a deep settling breath, Heck made his way to the rail beside the eerie man. "Near t'dusk, sir, an' a calm night looks ahead, I'd say."

The hooded head tilted slightly and Heck felt rather than saw those fishy eyes fixing on him. Repressing a sudden shiver, the swab leaned on the rail. "Ah, runnin' out a line, I see. Angry waters 'ere about, so I'm told. Sharks and dhenrabi. Makes fishin' a bit of a risk—you ever notice, did you, sir, that sailors nearly never fish? Just the passengers and the like. Odd, isn't it? I'd warrant it's t'do with the likelihood of us feedin' those fishes some day, which is a crawly thought indeed."

"Sharks," the man said in a high, thin voice.

Heck blinked, then frowned. "What's that? You fishin' for sharks? Oh, I sure 'preciate a sense of humour, I do. Sharks, ha. Looking to snag a big one, too, are ya? Like, maybe, one of those gold-backs that's as long as the *Suncurl* itself. Why, that'd be a fight or two, eh? You could lay bets who'd pull who aboard!" And he laughed, and kept laughing.

As long as his courage allowed, anyway, under that silent study from the shadowed face.

"Hah hah… hah… hah."

Light was fading. The man reeled out a few more loops of line.

Heck scratched at his stubbly jaw. "Sharks like meaty bait," he said. "Bloody bait. We ain't had fresh meat aboard since two days outa Moll. Whatcha using, sir? Had a nibble yet?"

The man sighed. "No. Yes, you say true. Bait needs to be bloodier."

"That it would, sir."

"And, perhaps, more substantial."

"Aye, I'd so wager. And a good-sized hook, too, why, a gaff-hook, in fact."

"Yes. Excellent notion. Here, hold this."

Heck found himself holding the bundle of line,

feeling the thrum of waves and depths as the trailing bait was tugged in steady rhythm. He turned to advise the guest that he was about to go on watch, but the man had wandered off.

He stood, wondering what to do. If the bell sounded and the fool wasn't back by then, why, he'd be in trouble, would Heck Urse.

Boots sounded behind him and with relief he turned. "Glad you're back, sir—oh, Captain!"

"What in Hood's name are you doing, Heck?"

"Uh, holding this line, sir."

"You are fishing."

"No sir! I mean, it was one of the guests! The fat one, he was fishing and he asked me to hold this until he got back, and I never had no chance to say I couldn't, cause of the night watch and all, so here I am, sir, stuck."

"You damned idiot, Heck. Tie it off in the rail. Then go wake up Birds and Gust, the sun's nearly down."

"Aye, Captain!"

ᔕ ᔕ ᔕ

"Last one I heard of was about twenty years ago, when I was upland in Theft so I never saw it for myself," Emancipor said, cursing his sudden sobriety which probably came from whatever Bauchelain had slipped into the tea he was now drinking. "They caught up to it down under the docks. The tide was out, you see—if it'd made water they'd have never gotten it and not a fisher boat would dare the bay for months, maybe years. Took twenty strong soldiers to kill it with spears and axes and the like, and even then only four walked away from the scrap."

"A formidable creature then," Bauchelain mused from behind steepled hands.

"Aye, and this one was only half a day old. They grow fast, you see, from eating their mothers."

"Eating their mothers?"

Emancipor glowered down at his tea. "No-one knows for sure, but the tale is like this. Jhorligg seeds swim the waters, like little worms. And if one finds a young woman in her time of bleeding—a conch diver or pearl swimmer or net crawler—why, that worm slides right on in, steals the womb, aye. And she gets big and big fast and then bigger still, and she starts eating enough for three grown men and keeps eating for six, seven months, until her skin itself starts to split. And then, usually on a moonless night, the Jhorligg rips its way free, straight through the belly, and eats the woman right there and then. Eats her all up, bones and all. Then down it races, for the water."

"Curious," Bauchelain conceded, "yet not as unlikely or bizarre as one might think. Parasites abound, and the majority of them dwell in water, both salt and fresh. Finding means of entry into hosts via any available orifice."

"Jhorligg just ain't beasts," Emancipor said. "Nearly as smart as us, it's said. They deliberately swim into nets and then curl up tight, until they're pulled aboard, then they tear loose and murder every fisher in the boat, eat them all. Some even use weapons, swords and the like lost overboard or thrown to the spirits of the sea. But Master, Jhorligg live in the shallows, coastal waters only. Never open sea. Never out here."

"Reasonable," murmured Bauchelain. "Too much competition in these waters, not to mention the risk of becoming prey. Now, Mister Reese, what you describe is a wholly marine creature that navigates on land only at birth, in the manner of turtles and dhenrabi. Yet is quite capable of lithe endeavours on a fisher boat's deck. By this, we must assume that it can survive out of water as necessity demands. But, I wonder, for how long?"

Emancipor shrugged. "It's said they look like lizards, but long and able to stand on their hind legs. Got a long sinewy tail, and two clawed arms, though it's said their bite is worst of all—can pull a man's

head right off and crunch the skull like eggshell…."
He trailed off then, as Bauchelain had slowly leaned
forward, eyes piercing.

"A most interesting description."

"Not the word I'd use, Master."

Bauchelain leaned back. "No, I imagine not. Thank
you, Mister Reese. I trust your senses have returned
to you?"

"Aye, Master."

"Good, set to my armour, then, and quickly."

"Quickly, Master?"

"Indeed. We are about to find ourselves on the
Red Road, Mister Reese. Tonight," he added as
he rose, rubbing his hands together, "shall prove
most fascinating. When you are done with the
armour, hone my sword—the red-bladed one, if
you please."

Armour? Sword? Emancipor felt his insides grow
watery with burgeoning terror, as he only now be-
came aware of the veritable cacophony of sounds
emanating on all sides. Groaning timbers, the squeal
of joins and click of shifting nails, the strange moans
and of things thumping alongside the hull, then slithering under to come round to the other side.

Suncurl pitched drunkenly, and darkness took the
sky beyond the lead glass porthole.

And somewhere down below, in the hold,

someone screamed.

〜 〜 〜

BENA YOUNGER HEARD THE TERRIBLE SHRIEK AND COWERED lower in the crow's nest.

Oh yes, my darling daughter, the night begins! Many are the terrible secrets of Laughter's End, an' could we fly wi' wings of black now's the time to leave the nest, dearie! But who in this world can flee their terrors? Hands o'er the eyes, ye see, and voices t'drown out all sordid griefs, an' the mind has wings of its own, aye, so beware the final flight! Into the abyss wi' all flesh left behind!

The stars swirled strange overhead and the *Suncurl* wallowed as if the wind had gasped its last. Black waves licked the hull.

But we are safe, darling, 'ere above the squalid fates. Like queens we are. Goddesses!

As yet another scream railed from the darkness below, Bena Younger realized that she did not feel like a queen, or a goddess, and this reach of mast and the nets of cordage creaking almost within reach did not seem nearly high enough for whatever horrors were unveiling themselves beneath the deck of the *Suncurl*.

While beside her, Bena Elder crooned and moaned

on, with hair standing on end and fluttering about, brushing her daughter's face like the wings of moths.

⇜ ⇜ ⇜

"WHO WAS DOING THAT SCREAMING?" HECK URSE demanded, reaching his lantern as far ahead as he could, the shadows dancing about the hull of the creaking ship, the rough, damp timbers of the ceiling brushing the top of his head. He peered into the gloom of the hold, sweat beading cold on his skin.

Others were awake now, but few had ventured beyond crowding the hatch leading from the crew's berths, and Urse recalled—with a sneer diffident in its bravado—seeing all those white rolling eyes, mouths open, round and dark like the tiny pocks in cliff walls where swifts nested. *Cowards!*

Well, they hadn't been soldiers, had they? Not a one of them, aye, so it was natural they'd look to Heck and Gust and Birds Mottle, not that any of them were quite free with their professions. No, such things came by obvious, in this hard confidence and the like when things were fast swirling down into some dark ugly pit. So here he stood, crowded by Birds and Gust both, with lantern in one hand and shortswords at the belts of the two soldiers at his back, Hood bless 'em.

"Briv's gone missing," Gust Hubb said, interrupting his endless praying to deliver this detail in a strained, squeaking voice. "Said he was coming down 'ere for a cask a something."

"Briv. Cook's helper?" asked Birds Mottle.

"No, Carpenter's helper."

"Was he named Briv too then?"

"He was, and so's the rope braider, named Briv."

Heck cut into this stupid conversation. "So Briv's gone missing, right."

"Carpenter's helper, Briv, aye."

"And he went down 'ere, right?"

"Don't know," Gust Hubb said. "I suppose he did if that was his screaming, but we don't know for sure now, do we? Could be one of the other Brivs doing the screaming, for all we know."

Heck turned round to glare at his one-eared companion. "Why would one of the other Brivs be screaming, Gust?"

"I wasn't saying one was, Heck. I was saying we don't know where Briv did the screaming, if any of 'em."

"Why does it have to be one of the Brivs doing the screaming?" Heck demanded, his voice rising in frustration.

Gust and Birds exchanged a glance, then Birds shrugged. "No reason, love."

"Unless," said Gust, "all three was going for the same cask!"

"That's not the question at all!" Birds retorted. "What's a carpenter's helper doing getting a cask of any kind? That's the question! Cook's helper, sure, makes sense. Even the rope braider, if'n he was looking—"

"She," cut in Gust.

"The Briv who braids ropes is a 'she'?"

"Aye."

"Well, my point was, you get wax in casks, right? And pitch, too, so there's no problem Briv the braider coming down here—"

"Listen to you two!" Heck Urse snapped. "It doesn't matter which Briv—"

There were shouts from the hatch above.

Gust snorted. "They found Briv!"

"But which Briv?" Birds demanded.

"It doesn't matter!" Heck shrieked. Then took a deep breath of the fetid air and calmed down. "The point is, nobody's missing, right? So who did that screaming we heard down 'ere?"

Gust rolled his eyes, then said, "Well, that's what we're down here trying to find out, Heck. So stop wasting time and let's get on with it!"

Heck Urse edged forward, pushing the lantern still further ahead.

"Besides," Gust resumed in a lower tone, "I heard a rumour that Briv the braider isn't Briv at all. It's Gorbo, who likes to dress up like a girl."

Heck turned again and glared at Gust.

Who shrugged. "Not too surprising, there's one of those on every ship—"

"And where did you hear that?" Heck demanded.

"Well, it's just a guess, mind. But a damned good one, I'd wager."

"You know what I wish?" Heck said. "I wish whoever cut off your ear hadn't cut off your ear at all."

"Me too—"

"I wish it'd been your tongue, Gust Hubb."

"That's not a nice thing to say, Heck. I wasn't wishing no-one cut off any part of *you*, you know. It still hurts, too. Stings fierce, especially now I'm sweating so much. Stings, Heck, how'd you like that? And then there's the swishing sounds. Swishing and swishing—"

"I'm going to go to the head," Heck said.

"What, now? Couldn't you have done that—"

"It's up there, fool! I'm going to check it, all right?"

Gust shrugged. "Fine by me, I suppose. Just make

sure you wash your hands."

ᛖ ᛖ ᛖ

"That scream wasn't no Jhorligg," Emancipor Reese asserted, licking suddenly dry lips.

Bauchelain, still adjusting the sleeves of his chain armour, glanced over and raised one brow. "Mister Reese, that was a death cry."

"Don't tell me Korbal Broach has—"

"Assuredly not. We are too far from land for Mister Broach to predate on this crew. That would, obviously, be most unwise, for who would sail the ship?" Bauchelain drew on his black chain gauntlets and held both hands out for Emancipor to tighten the leather straps on the wrists. "A most piteous cry," the necromancer murmured. "All foreseen, of course."

"Them nails, Master?"

A sharp nod. "It is never advisable to loose the spirits of the dead, to wrest them from their places of rest."

"It's kind of comforting to think that there are such things as places of rest, Master."

"Oh, I apologize, Mister Reese. Such places do not exist, not even for the dead. I was being lazy in my use of cliché. Rather, to be correct, their places of eternal imprisonment."

"Oh."

"Naturally, spirits delight in unexpected freedom, and are quick to imagine outrageous possibilities and opportunities, most of which are sadly false, little more than delusions." He walked over to his sword and slid the dark-bladed weapon from its scabbard. "This is what makes certain mortals so … useful. Korbal Broach well comprehends such rogue spirits."

"Then why are you all get up for a fight, Master?"

Bauchelain paused, eyed Emancipor for a long moment, then he turned to the door. "We have guests."

Emancipor jumped.

"No need for panic, Mister Reese. To the door, please, invite them in."

"Yes sir."

He lifted the latch then stumbled back as Captain Sater, followed by the First Mate, walked in. The woman was pale but otherwise expressionless, whilst Ably Druther looked like he'd been chewing spiny urchins. He stabbed a bent finger at Emancipor and hissed, "It's all your fault, Luckless!"

"Quiet!" snapped Captain Sater, her grey eyes fixing on Bauchelain. "Enough dissembling. You are a sorcerer."

"More a conjuror," Bauchelain replied, "and I

was not aware of dissembling, Captain."

"He's a stinking mage," Ably Druther said in a half-snarl. "Prob'bly his fault, too! Feed 'em to the dhenrabi, Captain, and we'll make the Cape of No Hope with no trouble in between—by the Storm Riders!" he suddenly gasped, only now seeing Bauchelain's martial fittings. Ably backed up to the cabin door, one hand closing on the shortsword at his belt.

Captain Sater swung round to glare at her First Mate. "Get down below, Druther. See what our lads have found in the hold—Hood's breath, see if they're even still alive. Go! Out!"

Ably Druther bared his crooked teeth at Bauchelain, then bolted.

Sater's sigh was shaky as she turned back to the conjuror. "What plagues this ship? It seems the air itself is thick with terror—all because of a single scream. Listen to the hull—we seem moments from bursting apart. Explain this! And why in Hood's name are you armed as if for battle?"

"Mister Reese," said Bauchelain in a low voice, "pour us some wine, please—"

"I'm not interested in wine!"

Bauchelain frowned at Sater, then said, "Pour me some wine, Mister Reese."

Emancipor went to the trunk where his master

kept his supply of dusty crocks, bottles and flasks. As he crouched to rummage through the collection, seeking something innocuous, Bauchelain resumed speaking to the captain.

"Panic is a common affliction when spirits awaken, Captain Sater. Like pollen in the air, or seeds of terror that find root in every undefended mortal mind. I urge you to mindfulness, lest horror devour your reason."

"So that scream was just some mindless terror?"

Emancipor could almost see the faint smile that must have accompanied Bauchelain's next words: "I see the notion of loosed spirits is insufficient to assail you, Captain, and I am impressed. Clearly you have an array of past experiences steadying your nerves. Indeed, I am relieved by your comportment under the circumstances. In any case, that scream announced the most horrible death of one of your crew."

There was silence then behind Emancipor and he lifted into view a bottle of black, bubbly glass, only to recoil upon seeing the thick glassy stamp of a skull on the body and a clatter of long bones girdling the short neck. He hastily returned it, reached for another.

"Spirits," said Captain Sater in a cold, dead tone, "rarely possess the ability to slay a living soul."

"Very true, Captain. There are, of course,

exceptions. There is also the matter of the Red Road, Laughter's End and its lively current. A most foul conspiracy of events, alas. To be more certain of what has awakened below, I must speak with my companion, Korbal Broach—"

"Another damned sorcerer."

"An enchanter, of sorts."

"Where is he, then? Not long ago he was on deck but then he vanished—I was expecting to find the creepy eunuch down here with you."

Emancipor found another bottle, the murky green glass devoid of scary stamps. Twisting round, he held it up to the lantern light and saw nothing untoward swimming in the dark liquid within. Satisfied, he collected a goblet, plucked loose the stopper and poured his master a full serving. Then paused and, with great caution, sniffed.

Aye, that's wine all right. Relieved, he straightened and delivered it into Bauchelain's left, metal-wrapped hand, even as the conjuror said, in a light manner, "Captain Sater, I advise you to refrain from voicing such gruff… attributions in your description of Korbal Broach. As Mister Reese can attest, my companion's affability is surely as much a victim of bloody detachment as was his—"

"All right all right, the man's a damned crab in a corner. You didn't answer me—where's he gone to?"

"Well," Bauchelain paused and downed a mouthful of the wine, "given his expertise, I would imagine he has…." And the conjuror's sudden, inexplicable pause stretched on, five, seven, ten heartbeats, before he slowly turned to face Emancipor. An odd fire growing in his normally icy eyes, the glisten of minute beads of sweat now on his brow and twinkling in his beard and trimmed moustache. "Mister Reese." Bauchelain's voice sounded half-strangled. "You have returned the bottle to my trunk."

"Uh, yes, Master. You want more?"

Trembling hand now, there, the one gripping the goblet. A peculiar, jerking step closer and Bauchelain was pushing the sword into Emancipor's hands. "Take this, quickly."

"Master?"

"A dark green bottle, Mister Reese? Unadorned glass, elongated, bulbous neck."

"Aye, that's the one—"

"Next time," Bauchelain gasped, his face flushing—delivering a hue never before seen by Emancipor—no, not ever on his master's normally pallid, corpulent visage. "Next time, Mister Reese, any of the skull-stamped bottles—"

"But Master—"

"Bloodwine, Mister Reese, a most deadly vintage—the shape of the neck is the warning." He was now tugging at his chain hauberk, seemingly in pain somewhere below his gut. "The warning—oh gods! Even a Toblakai maiden would smile! Get out of here, Mister Reese—get out of here!"

Captain Sater was staring, uncomprehending.

Taking the sword with him, Emancipor Reese rushed to the door and tugged it open. As he crossed the threshold Sater made to follow, but Bauchelain moved in a blur, one hand grasping her by the neck.

"Not you, woman."

That grating, almost bestial voice was unrecognizable.

Sater was scrabbling for her own sword—but Emancipor heard the savage tearing of leather and buckles even as the woman uttered a faint squeal—

And oh, Emancipor plunged out into the corridor, slamming the door behind him.

Thumps from the cabin, the scraping of boots, another muted cry.

Emancipor Reese licked his lips—yes, he was doing a lot of that, wasn't he? *Bloodwine, where have I heard that name before? Toblakai, said Master. Them giants, the barbaric ones. Tree sap, aye, mixed with wine and that's fair enough, isn't it?*

Rhythmic creaking and pounding now. Womanly gasps and manly grunts.

Emancipor blinked down at the sword in his hands. The overlong, near two-handed grip. The rounded silver and onyx pommel, well-weighted and gleaming as if wet.

Desperate cries moaning through the door's solid oak.

He thought back to that bottle's neck, then looked down at the sword's handle and pommel once more. *Oh. One mouthful? Just the one? Gods below!*

ᔐ ᔐ ᔐ

"You hear that?"

Birds Mottle squinted over at Gust Hubb. "Hear what?"

"Water. Rushing—I think we're holed!"

"No we aren't—feel it—we'd be sluggish, Mael's tongue, we'd be knee deep down here. We ain't holed, Gust, we ain't nothing so shut that trap of yours!"

They were whispering, since both understood that whispering was a good thing, what with Heck Urse creeping ever closer to the head in his search of whoever had done that scream and maybe finding what was left of the poor fool or even worse, nothing at all except maybe smears of sticky stuff that stank like wet iron.

"I hear water, Birds, I'd swear it. A rush, and clicks

and moaning—gods, it's driving me mad!"

"Be quiet, damn you!"

"And look at these nails—these new ones—look how they're sweating red—"

"It's rusty water—"

"No it ain't—"

"Enough—look, Heck's at the head."

That did what was needed in silencing Gust Hubb, apart from his fast breathing right there beside her as they crouched on the centre gangway running the length of the keel. Both strained their eyes at that wavering pool of lantern light fifteen paces ahead. They watched as the black, warped door was angled open.

Then Heck Urse's silhouette blotted out the glow.

"Look!" hissed Gust. "He's going in!"

"Brave man," Birds Mottle muttered, shaking her head. "I shoulda married him."

"He ain't that brave," said Gust.

She slowly drew her knife and faced him. "What did you just say?"

Gust Hubb caught nothing of that dangerous tone, simply nodding ahead. "Look, he's just peeking in."

"Oh, right." She sheathed her knife.

Heck leaned back and shut the head's door, then,

drawing his lantern back round, hurried back to where they waited.

"Nothing," he said. "No-one and nothing there."

Gust Hubb yelped and clapped a hand to the bandaged wound on the side of his head.

Heck and Birds stared at him.

"Something nipped me!"

"Something nipped what, exactly?" Heck asked. "It's a ghost ear now, Gust Hubb. It ain't there, remember?"

"I'd swear...."

"Your imagination," Birds Mottle said. Then she turned back to Heck Urse. "So what do we do now?"

Someone was coming up the walkway and they turned to see Ably Druther clambering closer.

"We did a search and all, sir," Heck said as the First Mate arrived. "Didn't find nothing and no signs neither."

Ably crouched, drawing them all into a huddle. "Listen, the whole damned crew is awake and eyes are rolling every which way—finding nothing won't work—"

"They do a count?" Heck asked. "Who's missing?"

"Rope braider Briv."

"Sure it was her?"

"That's what I was told. The short one with the orange hair and the stubbly legs—"

"Was Gorbo there?"

Ably Druther nodded.

Heck and Birds exchanged a glance. "You sure of that?" the former asked.

Ably Druther scowled. "Aye, he was the one reporting Briv missing."

Birds Mottle snorted. "Was he now?"

"I just said he was."

"And nobody else missing?"

"Well, just that fat passenger, the one always fishing."

"Ow!" Gust Hubb clapped a hand onto the bandage again.

"What's your problem?" Ably Druther demanded. "What's with the side of your head?"

"Didn't hear?" Birds asked, then continued, "Someone went and chopped off his ear—when he was sleeping, if you can believe that. And now it's a ghost ear."

"You can hear ghosts?"

The three ex-soldiers stared at the First Mate for a moment, then Heck Urse said, "That he can, only sometimes they take bites."

"What a horrible thing!" Ably Druther straightened and began backing away, fading with every step from the pool of lantern light.

Which was probably why none of the ex-soldiers crouched on the walkway actually saw whatever it was that rose up behind the First Mate and bit off his head.

⬿ ⬿ ⬿

LIKE A BLOT ON THE TURGID SEAS, THE DECK OF THE *SUNCURL* was a stain far below Bena Younger and her cackling mother. Edges blurred, the blackness itself the only proof that the ship existed at all, as the swirling thrusts of spume on the seas broke and rolled out to the sides, blooms of crimson-tinged luminescence cavorting away into the night.

Sails flapped as the *Suncurl* drifted as if indifferent to the wind, nudged along on the currents of the Red Road. No-one visible at the wheel. Only shadows caught in the rat-lines and rigging. No lantern swinging beneath the prow to light the way.

Close round the hatch to the hold huddled most of the crew. Reams of sand had been spread in a futilely protective circle, encompassing the hapless sailors, a detail that loosed hacking laughter from Bena Elder's gaping mouth.

Overhead, the fitful wind shredded rifts through

the thin shrouds of grey cloud, yet whatever world those rents revealed was naught but soulless darkness, bereft of stars.

Laughter's End exuded lifeless sighs into this turning, alien night sky, and Bena Younger crouched down, knees drawn up, arms wrapping them close against her chest, shivering in waves of blind, despairing terror.

Whilst her mother's desiccated head nodded in rhythmic reassurance, and she sang on in her crooning ways. *Lust and death this night, the murderous charade of love and treasures plundered! Oh, utopian circumstance as like a philosophe's wet aspiration—yes, all the dancers pause as if pinned through their free feet by dread spikes of reason! Exalted music of procreation! The Luckless fool has perchance undone us all—must we bless the sackless madman and his lurking lurker in the locked trunk? But no, warded indeed is that child—by none other that the one lost to all cogency!*

You and me, beloved, we shall survive this night, oh yes. Bena Elder promises! Safe from all hungry harm. Your dearest, loving mother is swelled to all decent proportions, for such are these exuding sighs that travel the Red Road, the whispered promise of rightful majesty accorded all things maternal, one hopes, and hopes, yes.

Cry not, daughter. Warm yourself in your mother's

unrelenting embrace—you are safe from the world. Safe and safer still. Virgin is your blood, virgin is your child mind, virgin yes, is the power of your soul—your sweetest kiss, yes, upon which the only one who truly loves you feeds, persists, endures.

You are mine ever and ever, even this night, and so I shall prove to all, no matter how hoary and dismal and desperate the challenge from below!

Let me sip each whimper from your lips, daughter. My strength grows!

⌒ ⌒ ⌒

ONE SCREAM. A SUDDEN WIDENING OF THE EYES, A FAINT primordial shiver. The soul tenses, crouches, awaits a repetition, for it is in repetition alone that a face is painted onto the dark unknown, a face indeed frightened, frightening, wracked with pain, or—and so one wishes—in bright, startled delight. But alas, this latter entreaty is yielded up so rarely, for such are grim truths unveiled, one beneath another and seemingly without end.

One scream. Breath held, heart stilled. What comes?

Now, an eruption of screams. From three throats. Well that is indeed … different.

The hammer and thump, the wild pitching of

inadequate light from somewhere down below. Boots on slick wood, the screams growing ravaged as tender tissue splits to the torrent of sound. And this, then, is the place and the moment when all totters on the knife-edge, precipice yawning, wind howling oblivion's flinty echo—does madness arrive? Unleashing misdirected violence and random calamity? Vague figures charging into one another, mouth-stretched faces crushed under heel, shapes pitching over the rail, bones snapping, blood gushing, grimy fingers digging into eyes—oh, so much is uttered by the fates to the chant of remorseless madness.

A deep, reverberating shout—nothing more would have been needed—a commanding voice to tug souls back from the brink.

If only one was there, among that huddle of crew, of the fortitude and iron spine to seize that one moment of salvation.

But terror had swum the night's sultry currents, seeping into flesh and mind, and now, in the wake of that terrible shrieking from below, chaos blossomed.

Life, as Bauchelain would well note—was he of any mind to voice comment—was ever prone to stupidity and, in logical consequence, atrocious self-destruction.

Of course, he was too busy spilling an endless

flood of seed into a barely sensate and in no way resisting Captain Sater down in his cabin, and this, as all well know, is the pinnacle of all human virtue, glory and exaltation.

∽ ∽ ∽

IN WILD WHIRLING LANTERN LIGHT ABLY DRUTHER'S headless corpse continued kicking even as blood gushed from the ragged nightmare that was his neck. His hands waved and twitched about as if strung to belligerent puppets. Birds Mottle, Gust Hubb and Heck Urse had collectively recoiled along the gangway towards the head—not Ably's, which had vanished, but the one at the bow—and in the process their feet had tangled, precipitating all three in a shrieking tumble down along one side of the mouldy hull, and there they thrashed, with Heck still holding the lantern high, in suddenly sodden clothes pungent with the reek of urine and, in Gust's case, something worse.

If the slayer now sought their souls, the harvest would have been virtually effortless. But nothing descended upon them, and apart from their screams, and the thumping of Ably's boots—and now, it must be added, the panicked thunder of feet from the deck overhead—there was no slithery, slurping rush to where they struggled and clawed, no hissing descent of slavering fangs.

Despite this, terror held the three ex-soldiers by their throats, especially when Ably Druther sat up, then twisted onto his hands and knees and jerkily regained his feet. Blood wept down his torso front and back, triggering in Heck's mind a dismayed revulsion that the man didn't even have the decency to use a napkin. Hands groping, Ably Druther took a step closer.

That step pitched him from the walkway and the trio of shrieks redoubled as the headless First Mate plunged down onto them.

Fingers snagged whatever they caught, and Gust wailed as his other ear was torn away from the side of his head, a blessing of symmetry if nothing else, but now terrible crunching, crackling sounds surged into his brain to war with the endless swishing of water.

Flailing, he scrabbled free from the corpse's reach, landing face first into the crevice between raised gangway and hull, only to find his gaping mouth suddenly filled with oily fur, squirming as he instinctively bit down even while gagging. A piteous squeal from the rat that ended on an altogether too high note as if bladders of air had been disastrously squeezed, and fluids most foul filled Gust Hubb's mouth.

His stomach revolted with spectacular effect, propelling the mangled rat a man's length out onto a tumbling landing on the walkway, where it came to rest on its back, tiny legs in the air, blood-wet slivery tongue lolling down one side of its open mouth.

Heck Urse, in the meantime, was being choked to death by a headless First Mate—who clearly wanted a head and any one would do. As a result, he forgot all about the risks of holding the lantern, electing in his extremity to use it as a weapon. In this, instinct failed him, since such a weapon was in truth likely only effective against the back of his assailant's head. A head that wasn't there. The hard, hot bronze of the lantern's oil-filled body cracked Urse in the face, igniting his beard and breaking his nose. Blinded, he flung the lantern away, spreading a flaring sheet of burning oil in its wake.

This elongated sheet of fire landed in between Birds Mottle's legs, as she was at that moment sitting up. As heat rushed for her nether parts, she kicked, lunging backward, to land skidding on the dead rat, all the way to the head which met her own with a solid crunch. Eyes pitching upward, she sagged unconscious.

Blood having distinguished his smouldering beard, Heck now had both hands on the lone hand squeezing his neck, and he began breaking fingers one by one. From Ably Druther came a series of anal gasps of, presumably, pain. And finally Heck Urse was able to twist free, clambering onto the First Mate's back where he pounded down on the corpse's back with futile abandon.

Gust Hubb loomed into view, his earless head ghastly in the flickering fire light, vomit slicking his chin to mingle with the blood streaming down both jaw-lines. Bulging eyes fixed on Heck Urse.

"Kill it! Kill it! Kill it!"

"I'm trying, you damned fool!" Heck retorted. "Get me a sword! A spike! Get me ropes, damn you!"

Gust Hubb scrambled past on the walkway. "Get it yourself! I ain't staying down here—no way—and I ain't ever coming down here again!"

Cursing, Heck reached for his knife. Still straddling the struggling body of Ably Druther, he twisted round and hamstrung the First Mate, one side, then the other. "Try walking now!" he snarled, then giggled, pushing himself back onto the walkway, yelping at the still-licking flames, then crabbing towards Birds Mottle.

"Wake up, love! We gotta get out of here—*wake up!*"

The third hard slap to the side of her face brought a flutter to her lids, then her eyes snapped open and she stared up at him, momentarily uncomprehending.

But Heck couldn't wait, and he began pulling Birds to her feet. "Come on, sweet. There's a demon or something down here—Gust's already bolted, the bastard—come on, let's go."

She looked at him blankly. "The ship's on fire. That's not good."

"We'll get the crew down here, every damned one of them, to put it out."

"Good. Yes. It's not good if everything catches fire."

"No, darling, that it ain't. Here, watch your step...."

⌒ ⌒ ⌒

WITH HECK URSE DRAGGING A MUMBLING BIRDS MOTTLE up the steep steps to the deck above, the headless corpse of Ably Druther was left more or less on its own, attempting to regain its feet but, alas, its legs had stopped working. Dejected, the First Mate sat down on the walkway, forearms resting on thighs and hands hanging down.

The spark of life could leap unfathomed distances, could erupt in places most unexpected, could indeed scurry along tracks of muscle and nerve, like a squirrel with a chopped tail. And sometimes, when even the life itself has fled, the spark remains. For a little while.

Once seated, Ably Druther ceased all movement, beyond a fainting slumping of the shoulders that quickly settled. Even the blood draining from various wounds finally slowed, the last drops thick and long.

Of the dread slayer, there was no sign.

The flames, which had been climbing the tarred hull, predictably eager, suddenly flickered, then guttered out.

And soft footsteps sounded, down the walkway from the head. Large, almost hulking, a figure wearing a full-length hauberk of black chain that slithered in the gloom. Bald pate a dull grey, thick-fingered hands reaching down as the figure crouched above the crushed body of the rat.

A soft whimper escaped Korbal Broach's flabby lips.

The very last rat aboard *Suncurl*. His most cherished, if temporary, servant. Witness to the monstrosity that had slain the First Mate with such perfunctory delight. And well *of course* the victim's head was missing. That made perfect sense, after all.

Korbal Broach paused, cocking a suitably attached ear.

The panic above seemed to have dwindled.

Perhaps the crew had abandoned ship, and oh, that would be regrettable. Surely neither the captain nor Bauchelain would permit such a thing. Did not Bauchelain know how Korbal so cherished these myriad pulses of sordid, not-especially-healthy lives? A harvest promised him, yes, once they were no longer necessary. *Promised.*

Why, Korbal Broach might have to pursue them, if truly they had fled—

A rasping cackle from the darkness—somewhere far down towards the stern.

Korbal Broach frowned. "Rude," he murmured, "to have so interrupted my precious thoughts. So rude."

The cackle crumbled into a rasp, and a voice drifted out. *"You."*

"Yes," Korbal Broach replied.

"No, it can't be."

"But it is."

"You must die."

"So I must. One day."

"Soon."

"No."

"I will kill you. Devour your round head. Taste the bitter sweetness of your round cheeks. Lap the blood in its round pool beneath you."

"No."

"*Come closer.*"

"I can do that," Korbal Broach replied, straightening and walking towards the stern. He passed beneath the grainy rectangle of lesser darkness that was the still undogged hatch. And in his mailed hand was a crescent-bladed short-handled axe that seemed to be sweating oily grit. Gleaming most evil.

"*That cannot hurt me.*"

"Yes, no pain. But I have no wish to hurt you." And Korbal Broach giggled. "I will chop you up. No pain. Just pieces. I want your pieces."

"*Bold mortal. We shall indeed test one another… but not right now.*"

Korbal Broach halted. The demon, he knew, was gone. Disappointed, he slipped the handle of the axe under his belt. He sniffed the air. Tasted the darkness. Listened to the slurp and swirl of water beyond the hull. Then, scratching his behind, he turned and began climbing the steps.

He never reached the top. But then, he had never intended to.

ᔧ ᔧ ᔧ

AT THE RUSH OF CHAOTIC COMMOTION ON THE MID-DECK of *Suncurl* immediately following the screams from below, Emancipor Reese crouched down in the doorway of the cabin hatch, stared out at the shrieking, hair-tearing, biting, clawing mob of sailors thrashing this way and that. Bodies plummeting over the rail. More screams rising up unabated from the hold's hatch. And he muttered, "Not again."

This was how the world circled round itself, curly as a pubic hair, plucked and flung wayward on whatever wind happened by as the breeches were tugged down and coolness prickled forever hidden places—as hidden as the other side of the moon, aye—and life spun out of control again and yet again, even as scenes repeated themselves, ghastly and uncanny—why, he half expected to hear the crunch of wood against rocks and ice, the squeal of horses drowning below decks, the staggering figures their faces blurring past in a smear of blood and disordered features. As the wind howled as if flinging darkness itself in all directions, a mad night's fit of murderous destruction.

But that, he reassured himself, was long ago. Another ship. Another life.

As for this, well.

Adjusting his grip on Bauchelain's oversized sword, Emancipor Reese straightened and ascended the steps onto the deck. He raised the weapon high. Then bellowed, *"Sailors abide! Abide! Abide for orders, damn you all!"*

Stentorian roars, as invariably erupted from officers in charge of things and the people working those things, could, if the fates so decreed, reach through to that tiny walnut-sized knob of civil intelligence that could be found in the brains of most sailors; could, with the Lady's blessing and Mael's drawn breath, shock into obedience those figurative nuts, and so deliver order and attentiveness—

"*It's Mancy the Luckless! He's to blame! Get him!*"

"Aw shit."

⤚ ⤚ ⤚

GUST HUBB, HAPLESS IN HIS EARLESSNESS, POKED HIS mangled head up from the hatch and, eyes bugging, was witness to a frenzied rush upon that manservant so aptly nicknamed the Luckless. Who happened to be holding an enormous sword which he began waving dangerously in an effort to hold back the snarling sailors. A belaying pin knocked the weapon from Mancy's hands and Gust saw the weapon cartwheel through the air—straight for him.

Bleating, Gust Hubb lunged back, and fire exploded between his eyes. Blood spurting everywhere as he brought his hands up to where his nose used to be, only to find two spraying, frothing holes. He fell to one side and rolled away from the hatch. The terrible smell of cold iron flooded up into his brain, overwhelming even the pain. This, commingled with the endless rush of water—which he now felt streaming from his half-blinded eyes—and some faint creaking from somewhere else, was all too much for his assailed senses and blessed oblivion swept in to engulf him in the black tide of peace.

For now.

Heck Urse, pulling Birds Mottle up into view, glanced over to see Gust lying motionless on the deck, his head resting in a pool of blood. Anger surged, white hot. He dragged Birds over the lip of the hatch and left her there, tugging free his short-sword that only a while earlier he had forgotten was even there.

A score sailors jostled around something at the base of the mainmast, lines rippling, then they were hoisting a limp body upward, scraping against the mast, arms dangling. Mancy the Luckless, beaten senseless and maybe worse, tied by one ankle, climbing skyward in ragged jerks.

"What in Hood's name are you doing?" Heck roared, advancing on the mob.

A woman named Mipple, her hair looking like a long-abandoned vulture nest, snapped her head round and bared stained teeth at him. "Luckless!

Tryin' to kill us all! We's sacrificing him to Mael!"

"Atop the mainmast? You fools, let him down!"

"No!" cried another sailor, waving a belaying pin and strutting about as if in charge.

Gust scowled at the man, trying to recall his name. "Wister, is it?"

"You ain't a man'o'the seas, Heck Urse—and don't go tryin' to tell us different! Look at you, you're a damned soldier, a deserter!"

"Mancy ain't got—"

"He cut off your friend's nose!"

Heck stopped, his scowl deepening. He wiped the blood from his own nose, heard a click. "He did?"

"Aye, with that big sword—the one jammed in the rail there—see the blood on the blade? That's Gust's blood!"

A chorus confirmed these details, heads nodding on all sides, manly sideways spits to punctuate Wister's assertions.

Heck slid his sword back into its scabbard. "Well then, hoist away!"

🌩 🌩 🌩

DARLING DAUGHTER, WHAT COMES? LISTEN TO THE SCRAPE *and bump, the creak and groan! Petard lofted the raving demon comes! No senses fired, reason's candle snuffed, make ready, my sweetness, and together we shall slit its throat wide and loose a rain of blood upon the fools below!*

The crow's nest pitched in gentle, vaguely circular motion, as all headway had been surrendered and *Suncurl* waddled in the swells, slowly edging cross-ways along the Red Road of Laughter's End. Figures still ran here and there below, as cries for the captain finally arose, then came the horrifying news of First Mate Ably Druther's brutal murder in the hold—by some beast unknown. A beast that could, Bena Younger heard, vanish into thin air. Panic was born anew once more on the deck below.

Trembling, she now found herself listening, breath held, as something bulky was being slowly hauled up the mast. All the way up, if her mother spoke true. A demon. Bena gripped ever tighter the small knife in her hand. Slit its throat, yes. With Mother's help.

Listen! Almost here!

∽ ∽ ∽

Sheathed in sweat, Bauchelain rolled off Captain Sater.

She moaned, then said, "Some mouthful."

He blinked away the sting in his eyes and regarded

her. "Most dire consequences follow imbibing Toblakai Bloodwine. I most humbly apologize, Captain."

"Done with me, then?"

"I believe so."

Armour, straps, fittings and underclothes were scattered all about the cabin. The lantern wick was dimming, oozing shadows into the corners, the light that remained singularly lurid. Somewhere nearby liquid dripped, a detail neither was anxious to pursue.

Sater sat up. "Do you hear something?"

"That depends."

"On deck—and we're drifting—no-one's at the wheel!"

As his gaze traveled over the captain's bared chest—he'd torn away her blouse in the first frenzied moments—the ample mounds swinging faintly then lunging as she reached for a scrap of clothing, Bauchelain felt a stirring once more. Grimacing, he looked away. "We were to discuss this fell night," he said, finding his quilted under-padding—one sleeve torn away at the seams—and pulling it on over his head. Pausing then to slick back his iron-hued hair.

"Ghosts," she snarled, rising to draw up her leggings, wincing with each tug.

"Not this time," he replied, combing through his beard. "A lich."

Sater stopped, stared across at him. "How in Hood's name did a lich get aboard my ship?"

"The nails, and perhaps something else. Korbal Broach no doubt knows more."

"And I'm sure I asked—earlier—where is he?"

"He walks the warrens, I expect. Likely hunting the creature through the maze of Hood's realm. A great risk, I might add. The Lord of Death holds no precious fondness for Korbal Broach."

She squinted. "Hood knows your friend ... *personally?*"

"Gods are easily irritated." Bauchelain lifted his hauberk, the chain flowing around his hands. "I must retrieve my sword. Should the lich stride in truth into our realm, here on this ship, well, we shall face a challenge indeed."

"Challenge?"

"Yes, in staying alive."

"It wasn't us!" she suddenly shouted.

Bauchelain paused, frowned at her. "You are hunted." Then he nodded. "As we suspected. What follows in our wake, Captain?"

"How should I know?"

"Describe your crime."

"That's got nothing to do with anything. It

wasn't even a crime. Not really. More like... opportunism."

"Ah, a sort of temptation to which one yields, casting aside all fear of consequences."

"Exactly."

"A momentary failing of ethics."

"Just so."

"Expedience winning its war with duty."

"So would we argue, yes—"

"A defense based on the weakness of nature belongs to untutored children and dogs that bite, Captain. You and your cohorts are all adults and if you relinquished your honour then fierce punishment is righteous and deserves a vast audience, a mob, if you will, expressing their most civilized glee over the cruel misery of your fate."

Her mouth hung open for a moment longer, then she reached for her sword and swiftly clasped the belt onto her pleasantly curved hips. "You're one to talk."

"Whatever do you mean?"

"Temptation and dogs that bite and all that. Damn you, I can barely walk. Do you imagine I take kindly to rape? I even tried for my knife but you twisted my wrist—"

"It is well known that Bloodwine—even in minute traces on my lips, or in my mouth—will effect a complimentary lust in the victim. Rape ceased as a relevant notion—"

"Doesn't matter when it ceased being whatever, Bauchelain! It's not like I consented, is it? Now for Hood's sake get your armour on—the weight just might hold you down—so I can start thinking straight—and don't worry, I won't cut your throat until we're out of all this."

"I did apologize," Bauchelain said. "Impulses beyond my control—"

"Better you grabbed your manservant—"

"Since I am not inclined that way I would have murdered him, Captain."

"We're not done with this."

"I dearly hope we are."

She marched to the door and flung it open, then paused at the threshold. "Wizard, can we kill this lich?"

Bauchelain shrugged.

"Oh, would that I could kill *you* right now."

He shrugged again.

⇜ ⇜ ⇜

As soon as the cabin latch dropped back down and the thump of the captain's boots hurried away, Bauchelain turned in time to see Korbal Broach stride out from a suddenly blurry back wall.

"Silly woman," the eunuch said in his reedy voice, heading towards his trunk. "Could she know the true absence of sexual pleasure—"

"Silly? Not at all. From shock to shame to indignation. She is right to feel offended, at me and at her own eager response. I am now considering a scholarly treatise on the ethical context of Bloodwine. Member emboldened by chemical means, desire like a flood, overwhelming all higher functions, this is a recipe for procreative and indeed non-procreative mayhem. It is a great relief to my sensibilities to know how rare Bloodwine is. Imagine a ready supply, available to all humans the world over. Why, they'd be dancing in the streets brimming with false pride and worse, egregious smugness. As for the women, why, pursued endlessly by men they would swiftly lose their organizational talents, thus plunging civilisation into a hedonistic headlong collapse of swollen proportions—rather, sizeable proportions—oh, never mind. Clearly, I will need to edit with caution and diligence."

Korbal Broach knelt in front of his trunk and flipped back the lid. Wards dispersed with minute breaking sounds, as of glass tinkling.

Bauchelain frowned down at his friend's broad back. "Humbling, the way you do that."

"Ah!" cried Korbal Broach as he leaned forward and stared down at his seething, slurping, burbling creation. "Life!"

"Is it hungry?"

"Oh yes, hungry, yes."

"Alas," observed Bauchelain, coming up to stand beside his companion and looking down at the monstrosity throbbing in its gloomy cave, a score of beady eyes littering up at him, "would that it could do more than heave incrementally in pursuit of prey. Why, a snail could flee it with nary shortness of breath and—"

"No more," sighed Korbal Broach. "Pleasant pastime. I harvested all the rats on board, yes?"

"So you did, and I wondered at that."

"Child is now propelled by a flurry of feet."

Bauchelain's brows rose. "You have melded rat appendages to your offspring?"

"Feet, limbs, jaws, eyes and spines and tails, yes. Child now has many, many mouths. Sharp teeth. A snivel of noses, a perk of ears, a slither of tails."

"Nonetheless, who would condescend to being gnawed to death?"

"Child will grow, clasping all to itself and so become more agile, larger, ever more hungry."

"I see. Is there a limit to its girth, then?"

Korbal Broach looked up and smiled.

"I see," Bauchelain said again. "Is it your intent to set your child in pursuit of the lich? Into the warrens?"

"Hunt," the eunuch said, nodding. "My child, freed to hunt!" He licked his thick lips.

"This will delight the crew."

"For a time," and Korbal Broach giggled.

"Well, I shall leave you to it, then, whilst I set out to find my sword—for the time when your child flushes our unwelcome guest."

But Korbal Broach was already mumbling rituals of sorcery, lost in his own, no doubt pleasant world.

⌐ ⌐ ⌐

EMANCIPOR REESE OPENED HIS EYES AND FOUND HIMSELF staring up at the horrid, desiccated visage of an ancient, toothless, nearly skinless woman.

"Aunt Nupsy?"

From somewhere nearby a thin voice cackled, then said in a rasping tone, "I have you now, demon. Slit your throat. Cut out your tongue. Twist your nose. Pluck your brows. Oh, pain delivered to start tears in your eyes and blood everywhere else! Agony and nerves afire! Who's Aunt Nupsy?"

Emancipor set his hand against the dead face

hovering in front of him and pushed the corpse away. It toppled to one side, folding in a clatter against a wicker wall.

"I'll get you for that! See this knife? An engagement with your navel! Hard about and cut your sheets, snip at the wrists and over the side—all hands on deck! Husbands are a waste of time so don't even think it! I bet she hated you."

Bruises, knobby bumps on the brow, gritty blood on the tongue, maybe a bruised rib or three, throbbing nose. Emancipor Reese tried to recall what had happened, tried to figure out where he was. Darkness above, a faint ethereal glow from the grey-haired corpse, swaying, creaking sounds on all sides, the moan of the wind. And someone talking. He twisted round onto one elbow.

A scrawny wide-eyed child huddled against a curved wicker wall, clutching a knife in her small, chapped hands. "Don't hurt me," she said in a mousy squeak. Then added, in that wise rasp he'd heard earlier, "She's not for you, oh no, demon! My teeth will leap at your throat! One by one! See that knife in my daughter's hands? It has drunk the life from a thousand foes!"

There was a rope tied round one of his ankles, the skin beneath terribly abraded. All his joints ached, leading him to a certain theory of what had occurred.

"I'm in the damned crow's nest. They strung me up, the bastards." He squinted across at the girl. "You're Bena Younger."

She flinched back.

"Easy there, I won't be hurtin' you. I'm Emancipor Reese—"

"Mancy the Luckless."

"Some things a man can't live down, no matter how lucky he is."

A cackle. "Lucky?"

"Gainfully employed, aye. Secure income, civil masters—why my wife must be dancing on the mound in our backyard, back in Lamentable Moll. My children worm-free at last and with clean, evenly waxed teeth and all the other modern conveniences. Aye, my ill-luck is long past, as dead as most of the people I knew back then. Why—"

"Shut up. The nails, fool, have twisted free. Spirits unleashed, wailing spectres and wraiths, yet one has risen, yes, above all the others. Clawed hands snatching. Souls grasped—oh hear their shrieks in the ether! Grasped, devoured, and the one grows. Power folded in, and in, layer upon layer, grim armour defying banishment—sweet in its multitude of nostrils the scent of mortal life, oh how it now hunts, to take all into its fang-filled, slavering, black-gummed and unpleasantly smelling mouth! Lo, I hear skull bones crunching, even now!"

"You addled, child? What is this old hag's voice that comes so wrongly from your young lips?"

Bena Younger blinked. "Mother," she whispered, nodding towards the corpse. "She speaks, she warns you, yes—why look upon me so strange? Why ignore her terrible glare so fixed upon you, sir? Bena Elder warns us—there is one below! Most terrible, oh, we have nowhere to go!"

Grunting, Emancipor Reese sat up and began loosening the knot at his ankle. "You've that right, Bena Younger. Nowhere at all." He knew to tread now with great care with the hapless girl, whose mind had so clearly snapped, imprisoned up here in this wicker basket with a mother who was weeks dead at the very least. The gulf of loneliness, of abandonment, had proved too deep, and into the cauldron of madness she had gone.

Bena Elder reappeared in the manner of suddenly bared teeth on her daughter's face. "Everyone shall die. Except me and my daughter—when the one comes, scaling the mast, and reaches so sure into this nest, it shall be *your* throat it shall grasp, Luckless. And we shall watch as it drags you over the edge. We shall hear the snap and crunch of your bones, the gurgle of your blood, the squishy plop of your eyeballs—"

"Think it won't smell you two up here? Your

daughter for certain, her life blood, the heat of her breath—all a tender lodestone to an undead—"

"I shall protect her! Hide her! In my embrace, yes!"

Emancipor struggled to his feet, leaned against the basket edge. "Might work. I wish you both the Lady's tug. As for me, I'm going back down—"

"You mustn't! Hear them down there! Insanity! And the one stalks, drinking deep on terror—"

And, as if to confirm the horror of all Bena Elder described, more shrieks from below. Renewed, re-doubled, repeated. Nether, despairing, primal.

The mast and crow's nest rocked as if buffeted by a giant's fist. Sharp, splintering sounds. They heard a yard slide from rings then crash onto the deck below.

"Hood's breath!" Emancipor gasped, clutching the edge, then twisting round and squinting down-ward. Shadows flitted here and there across the deck, more nightmarish than real. A body was sprawled near the hatch. There was no sign of what had struck the base of the main mast, but Emancipor could make out white lines to mark the splitting further down, almost luminescent against the tarred wood. "Something hit us down there, maybe even at the step down in the hold." He glanced back to warn Bena Younger of the risk, caught a blurred sight of a knife pommel, flashing for his head.

White light!

It's the bells, Subly! Can't you hear the damned bells?

Oh, wife, what did I do now?

⌐ ⌐ ⌐

BEAUTIFUL, THIS ROCKING MOTION, SO GENTLE, SO SOFT. Birds Mottle, whose left breast was a white sphere devoid of all pigmentation, in splendid, eye-widening contrast to her dark skin everywhere else, and hence her name's origin, a detail regretfully not as secret among the crew as she'd have wanted—but gods, trapped aboard with all these gruff sailors and the few women among 'em uglier than a priest's puckered arse, and well, what else t'do and besides, she was earning coin, wasn't she. Coin, aye, most useful, since who knew if they'd ever get away with what they were trying t'get away with. Birds Mottle, then, was reluctant to prise open her eyes.

Especially with all the screaming up near the foredeck. And was that a splat of blood or just a bucket of salt water, rivulets running down the steps now, maybe, and well there'd be no use to getting wet now, would there?

And so she opened her eyes. Sat up, found

herself facing astern, the cabin hatch slightly off to her right.

From which something wet, slick and murky was creeping into view, heaving over the steps. A chaotic scattering of small, black, beady eyes across a misshapen, mottled, lumpy surface. Slick, wet, yes, wetly slick, scrabbling and skittering noises as of minute claws on the wooden steps, faint slithering sounds, the pulse of organs now, throbbing beneath transparent, leaking skin. Half a face, below a purplish bulge that might be a liver, a glassy eye fixing on Birds Mottle momentarily before the next heave pitched the entire face down and out of sight.

Random locks of greasy hair, black and straight, blonde and curly, brown and kinked, each emerging from a seamed patch of native scalp. And was that a lone brow, arching now above no eye, arching indeed above what might be a gall bladder, as if gall bladders were capable of ironic, inquisitive regard, when everyone knew gall bladders could only scowl—

Birds Mottle then realized that she wasn't simply conjuring this slurping, twittering monstrosity out of her modestly equipped imagination. Oh no, this was real.

And it was flowing onto the deck, as if its bulk rode centipede legs, and eyes black and glittering that now, she was certain, glittered directly at her, rife with rodentian avarice. And was that a snaggle of toothy jaws, snapping and slavering above pink noses bent every which way though each lifted up to test the air cute as buttons while the jaws clacked and clicked ominous and minuscule?

Whimpering, she crabbed back across the deck.

A brawny human forearm flopped out from the apparition, from an inconvenient location, and on its wrist gleamed a vivid tattoo of gamboling lambs. A second arm pried loose from folds of organs, revealing a snarling black wolf tattoo. Nails popped off from fingers clawing along the deck as the thing dragged itself forward, intent as a giant slug bolting towards a lump of fresh dung.

Then all at once, its bulk was clear of the steps, and the enormous nightmare scuttled forward, shriekingly quick—as Birds Mottle proved with her open mouth and vocal chords seeking to shatter glass—and, twisting, round to gain her feet, she pitched sideways as her left hand and left leg both plunged into the hold hatch.

She vanished into darkness, bouncing once, twice along the length of the steep steps, and thumping heavily onto the gangway. A swirl of stars spun across her vision, corkscrewing into a burgeoning black maw, that then swallowed her up.

Beautiful, this rocking motion....

⌒ ⌒ ⌒

Captain Sater dragged an unconscious Mipple towards the foremast and left her propped there. Sater's longsword was in her gloved right hand. Spatters of blood streaked across the torn remnants of her blouse. Would that she had gone to her own cabin and strapped on her armour and maybe run a brush through her hair—which was what she normally did after sex, something about potential tangles and knots that could yank her head askew—but too late now and regrets were a waste of time.

Especially when that damned lich kept rising out of the solid deck to fold far too many withered limbs about sailors, dragging them back down amidst terrible screams—through splintering wood until all that remained was a hole no sane person could have thought a grown body could be pulled through. But they had been, hadn't they? Right down, the savage edges of wood gouging and tearing away chunks of muscle and shreds of skin and clothes.

And not once, pushing through the panicked mob, had she been able to reach them in time. In the gloom she had seen enough of this lich to know that her sword was likely useless against it. Half again as tall as a man, a massive, elongated melding of corpses wrapped in parchment skin. A dozen or more arms. Jutting, snout-like mouths emerging from shoulder, hip, back of neck, cheekbone. Red-rimmed, unblinking eyes gleaming dull from countless places. Each leg a conglomeration of many legs, the muscles all knotted like twisted braids, a ribcage thrusting forward box-like, with a solid rippled wall of ribs—and cutting through that would be impossible, she well knew. Even a thrust would be turned. And the head—was that Ably Druther's head?

But oh, how Sater wanted to start hacking off those damned arms.

Wister was crawling past in front of her, weeping worse than a babe in soiled diapers, dragging his belaying pin behind him like a giant rattle.

How many were left?

Sater looked about. Here on the foredeck, she saw, huddled a dozen or so. Six gaping holes exuded horror around them in a neat, even circle. The foremast itself had snapped its step somewhere below and now leaned to one side, rocking with each tug of wind against the few luffing, wing-flapping foresails somewhere above. If a gust hit them … damn, why did Ably have to get himself killed? That mast might just lift right up and out, or tear most of the foredeck with it as it toppled. Either way would be trouble, she suspected, and as captain she should be thinking about such matters—oh gods! Was she mad? A damned lich was eating her crew!

"Listen! Wister, get on your damned feet!" She pulled a ring of keys from her belt. "Weapons locker, floor of my cabin! Take Heck Urse—Heck! Never mind bandaging up Gust, he'll live—go with Wister. Break out the cutlasses—"

"Pardon, Captain, we don't have any cutlasses."

Sater scowled at Wister. "We don't? Fine, break out the truncheons, pins and the spears for propelling boarders—"

"We ain't got those neither."

"So what in Hood's name is in my weapons locker?"

"You ain't looked?"

Sater took a half step closer to Wister, the sword in her hand trembling. "If I knew, you brainless mushroom, I wouldn't be asking you now, would I?"

"Fine. Old Captain Urbot, he kept his private stock of rum down there."

Sater clawed at her face for a moment. "All right," she sighed, defeated, "break out the rum."

"Now you're talking!" Wister shouted, suddenly animated. "C'mon, Heck, you damned deserter! No time to waste!"

The two leaping down onto the main deck, boots

thumping, skidding, then returning just as fast. Wister's face was white as a churning chop. Heck's mouth worked but no sound came forth. Snarling, Sater pushed past them to the edge of the forecastle and looked down.

Something like an abattoir's rubbish heap was crawling across the mid-deck, just skirting the edge of the hatch. It had tiny eyes, dozens of them. And hundreds of short slithery tails snarling out behind it. Arms, partial faces, wayward locks of hair, scores and scores of tiny snapping jaws. It was, in truth, the stupidest monster she had ever seen.

With another snarl she leapt down onto the main deck, strode up to the thing and with one savage kick drove it over the edge of the hold hatch. A chorus of piteous squeals as the absurd mound of flesh plunged into the inky darkness. A splatting impact below and more squealing, and maybe a faint shriek—she couldn't be sure and who cared? Spinning round, Sater glared up at Wister and Heck Urse. "Well, what are you two waiting for?"

⤳ ⤳ ⤳

IN THE HOLD, NEAR THE HEAD, THE LICH WAS ARGUING WITH itself. Souls once bound to the iron nails that had been driven into their corpses, now reveled in the miasmic concatenation of flesh and bone that was the lich. The world was meat and blood and to be in the world demanded fashioning a likeness of the same. All too rare were those occasions when the ether was so saturated with sorcery that such conjuration was possible. Such luck!

To be meat and blood, one must devour meat and blood. Worldly truths, oh yes.

Fragments of identity persisted, however, each insisting on its right to an opinion, each asserting its claim to domination over all the others. And so voices tittered from the lich's various mouths where it stood amidst dismembered, half-eaten sailors, most of whom were dead. Voices, aye, yet one remained silent, ever silent, even as the argument continued to fill the shadows with a menagerie of once-selves.

"Merchant trader! Why, the hold's big enough, and if we eat all the sailors, why, the grand conjoining of spirit and flesh should prove more than sufficient to crew this modest ship!"

"An undead entrepreneur can only be some malevolent god's idea of a joke," said another soul in tones of gravel underfoot, and the strider of words ground remorselessly on, "Is this what we've come to, then, after countless generations of dubious progress? Your presence, Master Baltro, is an affront—"

"And yours isn't?" rasped a vaguely feminine

voice, and rasp was a truth indeed, if one were to take a sweet womanly utterance and run a carpenter's tool over it, should such things be possible and why not? "Sekarand did you in long ago and yet here you are again, chained to us goodly folk like a morally dissolute abscess—"

"Better than a wart!" shrieked the wizard who had been murdered by Sekarand in Lamentable Moll long ago. "I smell your reek, Hag Threedbore! Victim of disgruntled salamanders—no other possible explanation for your ghastly persistence—"

"And what of you, Viviset? Sekarand fed you into a tomb so warded that not even memory of you escaped! Why—"

"Please, please!" cried Master Baltro. "I must ask of you all—who else smells his own flesh somewhere nearby?"

A chorus of muted assents tripped from the lich's score mouths.

"I knew it!" shouted Master Baltro. "We must find—"

"As noble born," spoke someone else, "I must claim priority over the rest of you. We must find my self first—"

"Who in Hood's dusty name are you?"

"Why, I am Lordson Hoom, of Lamentable Moll! Related to the King himself! And I too sense the proximity of some crucial part of me—on this very ship!"

"Crucial? Well, that eliminates your brain, at least. I'd wager a pig-like snout."

"Who speaks?" demanded Lordson Hoom. "You shall be flayed—"

"Too late, fop, I already was and before the rest of you even ask, no, I'm not from Lamentable Moll. I don't know any of you, in fact. I'm not sure I even know myself."

"The nails—" began the once-wizard, Viviset, but the stranger's voice cut in.

"I'm not from any damned nails, but I swear I sensed the rest of you arrive. Including the one who refuses to speak and that refusal is probably a good thing. No, I think I was aboard long before any of you. Though exactly how long, I can't really say. One thing I can say: I preferred the peace and quiet before all you arrived."

"Why you inconsiderate snob—"

"Never mind him, Threedbore," Viviset said. "Look at the opportunity we now have! We're dead but we're back and we're all damned angry—"

"But why?" Master Baltro asked in his weedy voice.

"Why are we angry? You fool. How dare other people be still alive when we aren't? It's unfair! A grotesque imbalance! We need to kill everyone on board. Everyone. Devour them all!"

Souls yelled out in suddenly savage assent to such notions. Lips writhed with various degrees of muscular success in conveying their bloodlust, their hatred for all things living. All about the lich's misshapen, horrid body, mouths sneered, snarled, licked hungrily and blew kisses of death like lovers' promises.

At this moment something huge thundered down from the hatch, the impact reverberating the length of the keel. More voices cried out, these ones thinner, plaintive, pained. Then, in the relative silence that followed, came the snipping and clicking of jaws.

Viviset hissed in horror. *"It's that ... thing! The thing hunting us!"*

"I smell spleen!" squealed Lordson Hoom. *"My spleen!"*

At last, the silent one, whose silence had been, in truth, the fugue of confusion, the incomprehension of all these strange languages, finally ventured its opinion on matters. The Jhorligg's bestial roar sent selves tumbling, flung about in the cold flesh and cooling blood threads of the lich's manifold body. Stunning all into mute terror.

Mostly incoherent thoughts from the Jhorligg thrashed with the fury of a storm. *Eat! Rend! Flee!*

Breed! Eatrendfleebreed! And up rose the eleven arms of the lich, torn, bloody fingers bending into rending positions, tendons taut as cocked crossbow cords. Weapons readied, the creature spinning round to face the monstrosity now crawling ever closer up the length of the wooden walkway.

That monstrosity was dragging something. Something that kicked booted heels against the hull. Kicked and scraped in frenzied panic.

"My spleen!" cried Lordson Hoom again. *"It wants to eat me!"*

⌒ ⌒ ⌒

"LIFE IS LIKE A CLAM," BIRDS MOTTLE'S FATHER ONCE TOLD her. *"Years filtering shit then some bastard cracks you open and scrapes you into its damned mouth. End of story, precious pearl, end of story."*

They'd lived by a lake. Her father had fought a lifelong war with a family of raccoons over the clam beds he'd staked out, run fences and nets round, and done just about everything else he could think of to keep the masked thieves from his livelihood. In terms of intelligence and raw cunning, the raccoons had old Da beat, and they drove him both mad and into his grave.

Birds Mottle, who'd had a much sweeter name

back then, found herself—as she stared down at the lifeless face of her father, the expression all twisted by that last scream of outrage—contemplating a future comprised of the war that had killed Da. Her sole inheritance, this feud she could not hope to win. What kind of life was that?

Why, it was filtering shit, wasn't it?

Fifteen years old at the time, she'd collected a small pack full of things from the shack that stood on rickety stilts on the mud-flats—home—and set out for Clamshell Track, walking one last time that desultory route into Toll's City where they'd once hawked their harvest. Not much of a city, Toll's. The inner wall marked the modest extent of the town of twenty years past, and as for all the new buildings that rose outside the fortifications, well, not one stood more than two storeys tall.

Take a stick and jam it deep into the mud, just up where the waves reach on an easy day. Come back a week or two later and there's a mound of silts gathered round the stick on one side, and a faint shallow pit on the opposite side. Unless a storm arrives to drag the stick away, the mound grows, the hole slowly fills in.

That was Toll's City. A stone keep in the middle for the stick, the slow even drift of people from the countryside, silting up round the keep the way people did. A decade or so of miserable warfare, forcing the building of defenses, and then a time of *"the drudgery of peace,"* as the soldiers said to describe all those bells of wasted training and standing sentinel over borderlands no-one gave a damn about.

She didn't mind becoming a soldier. She didn't mind the half-mad fools she'd been squad-mates with. Gust Hubb, Bisk Flatter, Sordid and Wormlick. And, of course, Heck Urse, the one she'd ended up taking to bed, as much from boredom as lust—although, and this was indeed a truth—boredom's best answer, every time, was flat out rutting, grunting, frenzied lust. Why, there was a world of married or otherwise committed women bored out of their skulls, when the obvious solution was right there in front of them. Or the hut down the road.

Too bad they'd lost Bisk, Sordid and Wormlick that night. And now maybe it'd all been an accident, the way the other dory popped a knot belly-deep in the trough, sucking itself and its three wailing soldiers right down to the bottom, where the riptide grabbed all it could on its rush back to deeper water. And maybe it was just the Lady's pull'o'luck that the rest of 'em, Sater and Ably included, were in the bigger boat, the one with all the loot, that made it out to the *Suncurl* where it strained its fore and aft anchors in that churning tidal flow in the cut.

And maybe even Sater had been telling the truth about that haul. Toll's own mintage, silver and gold not yet grimed by a single grubby hand, aye, in bound stacks—well, she'd seen those, hadn't she? Seen and heaved up from the boat, o'er the rail and into Ably's waiting arms, the weight of wealth, so much wealth. But what about that other stuff? The burlap-wrapped, bulky objects, massively heavy, with knobs protruding, stretching the ratty fabric? Big as idols, swear up'n down, not that Toll's City had much in the way of stupid-rich temples, like the ones she'd heard about from Bisk—who'd lived up in Korel and only escaped time on the Wall by turning in his kid brother. Huge temples, with thousands of poor people coughing up their last coppers into the big bowls even as they reeled glass-eyed from any of a dozen plagues that seasonally tore through the shanty-towns. Rich enough, oh yes, for bloody idols and inset gems on those collecting bowls, and stealing from those soul-eating oh-so-pious crooks was just fine by her, and would've been, too, if that's what they'd done and if those were what those wrapped-up things were, which they weren't.

Half the city's coinage, aye, the hoarded loot of the Chanters—that nasty mob of tyrants ruling the roost—all to buy the services of that cursed mercenary company, them Crimson Guard, and why'd they needed 'em? The unification of all Stratem, oh yes, with Toll's City as the blustery capital. An end to skirmishes and feuds, to trader wars between damned factors out in the bush, to ambushes of furbacks and caravans of pelts burnt to a crisp just to make someone's neighbour starve, babes and old alike and all in between, too. Mercenaries, yes, to deliver the drudgery of peace.

Imagine, then, arriving at the coast where it was said the damned Crimson Guard had landed by the hundreds, only to find the fools gone. Shipped back out, on their way somewhere else, and in a hurry, too.

Well, turn round and take it all back home?

Sater had a better idea, aye.

Maybe better. Maybe Birds Mottle wasn't so sure anymore, now that she was embedded, head, shoulders and at least one tit, within a nightmare blob of squishing, squelching, wheezing, twittering, gasping, blinking and mouthing and throbbing … *thing*.

Embedded, aye. And more. Merged. Melded. Each breath a slimy inhalation of bright, cool liquid—air? No, wasn't that. Spit? Could be, but spit brimming with whatever was in air that kept people alive. Blood? No, too thin. Too cool.

Eyes open, seeing red, mostly, and some pulsing

arteries or veins. Not even blinking anymore, since more cool liquid, yellowy perhaps, but thin as the lid on a snake's eyeball, kept everything from drying out.

Embedded, the monstrosity dragging itself forward and dragging her in its wake. She struggled to get to her feet, so she could stand—but that wasn't possible, she suspected—she'd never be able to lift this damned thing, not even in her arms much less tottering above uncertain footing.

Oh, what a lousy way to die. What a lousy way to stay alive, in fact. Dead would be good, yes, good indeed.

⌐ ⌐ ⌐

LIKELY UNNOTICED BY ANYONE, BAUCHELAIN HAD EMERGED onto the mid-deck, found his sword jammed by one edge into the rail off to his left—another hand's length and the precious weapon would have gone over the side. Blood gleamed on the reddish-black iron. Tugging it free, he paused, glanced astern.

Something....

Curious, Bauchelain ascended the aft steps to the wheel deck. No-one had tied off, leaving the rudder to flap and swing, turning the huge wheel every which way. Frowning, indeed disappointed by such sloppy seamanship, he continued on to stand at the stern rail. Looked out over the gloomy Red Road of Laughter's End.

Crimson swirl, crimson phosphorescence, the wake jagged and random. He saw a faint carved trough, then noted the fishing line looped and knotted at the rail. They were trailing bait, possibly an unwise notion given the circumstances. Likely Korbal Broach's doing. He stroked his beard, musing.

Commotion from the bow. Turning, Bauchelain squinted. The lich had struck again, the Jhorligg's mindless hunger staining every soul with its desperate need. Misapprehension was ever a curse among the undead, alas. Although, given the emboldened strain of raw power curling through the currents on these seas, even misapprehension could acquire a certain… corporeal truth.

The lich devoured. And so grew in mass, in strength. A most curious evolution, quite possibly unique. Without doubt worthy of further study.

A final shriek wavered up from the latest victim.

Thrumming, as of a bass lyre's string being plucked, drew him round once more. The fishing line was sawing back and forth, proof that something had been caught on the hook. A shark? Perhaps.

The line suddenly went slack.

Snapped? Most likely.

He saw dorsal fins in their wake, cutting the red-black water, rushing fast, then out, sweeping round the ship. Scores and scores. One of the sharks broke the surface barely a knife's throw from the rudder—a creature two-thirds the length of the *Suncurl*. It twisted to avoid colliding with the stern, then slid past, buffeting the hull, its shiny buckler-sized eye flashing. Then plunged from sight.

The sharks, Bauchelain realized, were fleeing.

Well, these waters were indeed thick with dhen-rabi—and there was one of the gargantuan segmented behemoths, breaching a huge, rolling swell a thousand strokes to the east. Astonishingly fast, he observed. Outracing even the sharks....

Bauchelain finger-combed his beard some more.

∽ ∽ ∽

GAUZE SWADDLED GUST HUBB'S FACE JUST BELOW HIS EYES and wrapped round his head in a thick band, the sun-bleached white material marred by three dark red blooms, one centre, the other two flanking at more or less the same elevation.

Noises assailed him. Chittering, snapping of jaws from one side, swirling water from the other. This was manageable, or so he had just concluded when, from the watery side, there came a devastating crunch and then vast, unbearable pain. The sudden assault was of such force that he bit down on his tongue and now there was even more blood, spurting from his mouth.

He had been kneeling on the foredeck, staring accusingly at everyone else, all of them mocking him with their perfect faces, their rosy noses and squid-hued ears all perfect in their delicate folds and cute lobes. But now he toppled to one side, curling up as agony tore through him from an ear he didn't even own anymore.

And now nipping bites affronted his other missing ear and this, dammit, was very nearly the worst night of his life.

Heck Urse crawled over, brandishing a knife and Gust recoiled upon seeing it.

"Idiot, I ain't gonna cut you or nothing! This is protection, for when that lich pops up again—gods, you'd think its belly was full by now. Look at Mipple, she's only now come round—missed all the fun, didn't she? I hate it when people do that. Anyway, I come to give ya this—" and he showed his other hand, this one gripping a clay jug. "Rum!"

⌒ ⌒ ⌒

CAPTAIN SATER DOWNED ANOTHER MOUTHFUL, THEN FLUNG

the empty flask to one side. Where had it all started to go wrong, she wondered. Sure, stealing a half-dozen Sech'kellyn statues was probably a bad idea, the way tales of terrible curses swirled around the damned things. They'd been found buried in a neat little row beneath the foundation rubble of Avoidance Alley just behind Toll's Keep, ghastly squatting figures of some foreign, chalk-white marble now stained and mottled by a century or two of kitchen refuse and royal sewage. The expressionless, gaunt faces were all the more chilling for their black iron eyes and black iron canines—seemingly immune to the ravages of rust—and their strange limbs with too many knobby joints, the twice bent knees framing the forward-thrusting heads, the raptor-like, elongated fingers and, most peculiarly, iron collars enclosing their thin necks, as if the six creatures had been pets of some sort.

The court mage—calling them Sech'kellyn, whatever that meant—had claimed them at once, and Sater herself had been among the hapless fools lugging the things up to the sorcerer's beehive apothecary perched atop the city's lone hill. A week later she'd helped carry them back to the keep, down into some long unused storage room barred by a newly installed iron door into which the mage gouged so many warding glyphs and sigils the door looked like a flattened crane nest by the time he was done.

The poor sorcerer went mad shortly thereafter, and if there was some kind of connection then no-one official wanted to talk about it. Sater hadn't been alone in paying coin for a ritual cleansing at Soliel's Temple behind Cleanwater Well—every other soldier who'd set hands on those statues had done the same, with the exception of Corporal Steb, who'd been picking his nose with a dagger point and, walking up to a door that suddenly opened, drove the point into his brain—amazing the dagger ever found it, truth be told. But then, things had mostly settled and it looked as if they'd escaped whatever curse there'd been. When the mage drowned himself in a bowl of soapy water, well, he'd been mad by then, hadn't he, so it was no real surprise.

Some bright wick had then decided to offer them as gifts to the Crimson Guard—who were, it was said, deep into the arcane stuff anyway. But maybe, Sater now wondered, they'd been less a gift than a not-so-noble desire to get rid of the ugly things.

So then she went and stole them. Why? What insane impulse had taken her then, like a bony hand round her throat? Over the side they shoulda gone, aye, right over the side.

Was it the curse that had conjured to life the miserable lich?

She needed to get rid of them. Now, before it was too late—

An eruption of screams from below—so awful that even her rum-heated blood went icy cold—and the thunder of some collision, as of two massive forms slamming into one another, and the entire ship shivered. More screams, the thumping of blows delivered with savage strength and ferocity.

With hammering heart, Sater glared around, saw a trio of sailors crowded up at the prow. "Briv! And you too, Briv! And you, Briv! You three, here, take my strongroom key—"

"*Down below?*" one of them shrieked.

"At the stern and it's all quiet there. There's six wrapped statues—I want 'em up here, understand? Up and o'er the rail! Quick!"

All at once a figure was standing at her side. Tall, hulking, a flabby, round, child-like face peering down at her. The thick lips licked beneath bright, beady eyes. "Statues?"

⟜ ⟜ ⟜

BRIV, COOK'S HELPER, GLANCED OVER AT BRIV, CARPENTER'S helper, then back at a snuffling Briv, Rope Braider, whose orange mane of hair was strangely tousled, almost askew. He saw terror writ plain on their faces, as much as he himself must be showing on his own. Descending the steps in front of them was the scarier of the two passengers (three if counting the manservant but nobody ever counted the manservant), the oversized one with the round face and thick lips and tiny voice.

Seemingly completely unafraid, which meant he was insane.

Their escort to the strongroom, rustling in full-length chain beneath a thick woollen black cloak. Pudgy, pale hands folded together like he was a damned mendicant or something.

We're all going to die. Except maybe him. That's how it always is. People in charge always survive, when everyone else gets slaughtered. No, he'll live, and so will Cook, because no-one likes to cook and that's just the thing. Cook's a poet.

No, really, a poet. He sure as Hood ain't a cook.

Now if only he was any good at poet stuff. Can't sing, can't play an instrument, can't make a rhyme because rhyming, well, laddie, it's beneath him.

"I dreamed this thing
This thing of dreams
An army marching close
Each soldier cut off
At the knees
Which was strange and all

Since they were
Foot-soldiers."

Aye, Cook's latest, his morning paean to the slop he shoveled into the bowls. That pompous face and that rolling cadence, as if the tumbling refuse of words coughed out from his throat was some kind of profound thing—why, I've read poetry, oh yes, and heard plenty too. Said, sung, whined, gargled, mewled, sniffed, shouted, whispered, spat. Aye, what seaman hasn't?

But what do we know? We're no brush-stroked arched brow over cold, avid eye, oh no. We're just the listeners, wading through some ponce's psychological trauma as the idiot stares into a mirror all love/hate all masturbatory up'n'down and it's us who when the time comes—comes, hah—who are meant to gasp and twist pelvic in linguistic ecstasy.

Yeah, well, Cook can stroke his own damned ladle, know what I mean?

Briv, Carpenter's helper, gave him a nudge. "Get on wi'ya."

"Leave me be," snarled Briv, Cook's helper. "I'm going, all right?"

And down they went, the steep steps, down into the hold, where horror did abide—up near the head, that is. And all three seamen (or two seamen and one seawoman who was, in fact, a seaman), desperately needed to go to the bathroom.

⮌ ⮌ ⮌

Briv, Carpenter's helper, stayed one step behind Briv, Cook's helper, and one step ahead of Briv, Rope Braider, who, if she braided ropes as bad as she did her hair, would probably better serve the ship as Cook. Since Cook was a poet.

But then, without a rope braider, things would get unraveled and that wouldn't do. And listen to those demons scrapping near the bow—if he bent right down to look between his own ankles, through the gap in the steps, he might see something of that snarling, hissing, snapping, thumping battle. But what good would that do him, hey? None a whit. They was just up there bashing the precious hull, bruising the wood, punching out the caulk and gouging nasty gouges and if reefs and shoals and rocks and deadheads weren't enough trouble, here they had unmindful demons doing all kinds of damage.

Now, if Carpenter had knowed his business, well, it'd be all right, wouldn't it? But the man was a fool. Killing him had been a gift to the world. Funny, though, how that one death-cry seemed to unleash all the rest of what showed up and now people were dead everywhere and there, see, that was Ably Druther, his body at least, sitting there barely a nail's throw behind the steps. Sitting like he was just waiting for his head to come home. Looked crazy upside down like this, and whatever fought in the gloom further up, well, that was blessedly hard to make out—

"Damn you, Briv," hissed Briv, Rope Braider, "you tryin' t'catch your own shit in your mouth or something?"

"You don't sound ladylike," Briv replied, straightening up then hastening two steps to catch up to Briv, Cook's helper. "We shoulda brought a lantern."

The giant eunuch was down on the walkway now and not waiting courteously for the sailors to join him, just heading on sternward to the strongroom. Briv, Cook's helper, should never have given the hairless freak the key. Why, Briv, Carpenter's helper, could have stood up to him easily enough—

"Ow! You're treading on my heel, woman!"

"There's a headless guy sitting behind me, so hurry on, Briv!"

"He's not paying you any mind."

"There's eyes on my backside, I'd swear it."

"Not him, if you turned his head it went and fell off."

"Look, a woman knows these things. When someone's giving 'em the up down left right. Worse on a ship, too, all these letches."

"Lich, not letch."

"How do you know? Anyway, since I'm the only decent female aboard, it's all on me, you know."

"Who's all on you?"

"Wouldn't you like to know."

"Not really. Just curious." And, maybe, aghast, but it paid a man to be polite to a woman. Even one whose breasts seemed to float up and down like cork and twine buoys on a swell.

The eunuch had halted before the strongroom door.

Briv, Briv and Briv crowded up behind him.

"Is this a good idea?" Cook's helper asked as the eunuch slid the key into the lock.

"Ooh," sighed Rope Braider.

Key turned. Tumblers clicked.

"Is this a good idea?" asked Cook's helper once again.

⌐ ⌐ ⌐

SECH'KELLYN WERE BAD ENOUGH. BUT SECH'KELLYN wearing ensorcelled collars, well, that boded ill indeed. Homunculi, of sorts, Sech'kellyn were Jaghut creations, modeled—it was said by the scant few with sufficient authority to voice an opinion—on some ancient race of demons called the Forkassail. White as bone, too many knees, ankles, elbows, even shoulders. Being perfectionists of the worst sort, the Jaghut succeeded in inventing a species that bred true. And, even more typical of Jaghut, they went and made themselves mostly extinct, leaving their abominable conjurations free to do whatever they pleased, which was usually kill everyone in sight. At least until someone powerful showed up to hammer them back down and chain their life-forces and then maybe bury them somewhere nobody would ever disturb, like, say, under a poorly made alley in a fast-growing city.

A powerful enough sorcerer could subsequently reawaken the geas on such creatures, could indeed bind them to his or her will, for nefarious and untoward purposes, of course.

Perhaps this was what had been done to the six Sech'kellyn in the strongroom.

But in truth, it was nothing like that at all.

It was much worse.

Oh yes.

⌐ ⌐ ⌐

Wizards delegate. One could always tell the wizards who did by the way they sat around in their towers day and night concocting evil schemes of world domination. Somebody else was scrubbing out the bedpan. Wizards who didn't delegate never had the time to think up a black age of tyranny, much less execute what was necessary to achieve it. Dishes piled up and so did laundry. Dust balls gathered to conspire usurpation. Squirrels made the roof leak and occasionally fell down somewhere in the walls where they couldn't get back out and so died and then mummified displaying grotesque expressions after wearing their teeth out gnawing brick.

Mizzankar Druble of Jhant—which had been a city on Stratem that fell into dust centuries past and the presence of which was not even guessed at by the folk of Jatem's Landing, a new settlement not three thousand paces down along the very same shore—Mizzankar Druble of Jhant, then—who had been, it was agreed by all now long dead, a most terrible sorcerer, a conjuror, an enchanter, a thaumaturge, and ugly besides—Mizzankar Druble of Jhant, aye—who'd raised a spire of gnarled, bubbly black, glassy stone all in a single night in the midst of a raging storm which was why it had no windows and the door, well, it was knee-high and about wide enough for a lone foot as if that made any sense, since Mizzankar was both tall and fat so everyone who was now dead decided he must have raised that tower from the inside out, since the poor fool ended up stuck in there and Hood knew what terrible plans he was making which more than justified piling up all the brush and logs and such and roasting the evil wizard like the nut in a hazel—Mizzankar Druble, of Jhant, yes, he had been a wizard who had delegated.

Like hounds needing a master, the Sech'kellyn were demanding servants. And as such, the task was indeed full time and not much fun either. Mizzankar Druble—who in truth had been a minor wizard with the unfortunate penchant of attempting rituals far too powerful to control, one of them resulting—in a misjudged battle with an undead squirrel—in the explosive, terrifying eruption of molten rock that rose all round him where he stood in his pathetic protective circle—thus creating a towering prison he never did escape—but Mizzankar Druble, wise enough to delegate, and happily possessing six demonic servants hatefully created by some miserable Jaghut, understood—in a spasmodic moment of clarity—the need for a powerful, preferably enormous, demon that could assume the burden of commanding the Sech'kellyn.

In the most ambitious and elaborate conjuration of his life, Mizzankar summoned such a creature, and naturally got a lot more than he bargained for. An ancient, almost forgotten god, in fact. The battle of wills had been pathetically short. Mizzankar Druble, of Jhant, had, in his last few days of life before the villagers roasted him alive, been set to the task of scrubbing bedpans, rinsing dishes, wringing laundry and chasing dust balls on his hands and knees.

Gods, even more so than wizards, understood the notion of delegation.

Now the tale of the god's subsequent adventures, and all relating to the Sech'kellyn and the tumbling disasters that led to their theft and burial in what would one day be Toll's City, is a narrative belonging to someone else, at some other time.

The vital detail was this: the god was coming for his children.

∽ ∽ ∽

BLEARY-EYED, HALF-CRAZED WITH THROBBING PAIN IN numerous parts of his head, Emancipor Reese, Mancy the Luckless, clawed his way onto his knees, then paused while everything reeled for a few dozen heart-beats. His face pressed against the damp wicker, his gaze shifted so that his left eye took in Bena Young-er—crouched once more opposite him, knife raised in case he should lunge murderously her way—but of course that wasn't likely. He might lunge indeed, but if he did it would be to heave out whatever was left of Cook's dubious supper, and the thought of that—a most satisfying image dancing in his mind's eye of the vicious child covered in fetid slop—while satisfying on one level, thrummed a warning echo of blistering pain through his skull.

No, too much action demanded by such explosive, visceral expression. He closed his eyes, then slowly edged up a little further, until his head cleared the basket's tattered edge. Opened his eyes again, blinking smartly. Emancipor Reese found himself looking astern.

Still night? Gods, would it never end?

Black looming overcast blotting out everything above the murky rolling seas. Dhenrabi breaching the surface on all sides, racing faster than any ship. Damn, he'd never seen the behemoths move so fast.

Somewhere below a fight was going on, sounding entirely unhuman, and reverberations thundered through the ship, rocking the mast with each blow against the hull.

Another massive bulge in the water, this one directly behind the *Suncurl*, swelling, rising, looming ever closer. And Emancipor now saw Master Bauchelain, standing wide-legged a couple strides back from the aft rail, sword held in both hands, eyes seemingly fixed on that surging crest.

"Oh," said Emancipor Reese.

As two enormous, scaled arms thrust up from the foaming bulge, crashing down in a splintering, crushing grip on the rail—wood snapping like twigs—the long, curved talons plunging into the aft deck. Then, in a massive heave of cascading water, the elongated reptilian head reared into view between those arms. Maw open, articulated fangs dropping down as water slashed out to either side.

The entire ship stumbled, hitched, seemed to stagger into a deathly collapse astern—the prow lifting high—as the apparition pulled itself aboard.

And all of it—the entire scene with creature and Bauchelain, who now leapt forward, sword flashing—raced fast towards Emancipor as the crow's nest and the mast to which it was attached, pitched down. Something slammed into Emancipor's back, driving all the air from his lungs, and then a scrawny body, wailing, was rolling over him, out into the air—ratty hair and flailing limbs—and he threw himself forward, reaching—

⋙ ⋙ ⋙

THE SUDDEN LIFT OF THE PROW FLUNG LICH AND MISSHAPEN child down hard, collapsing the planks of the o'er keel gangway. At this moment, unfortunately for the child of Korbal Broach's unnatural procreation, the lich was on top. Crushing impact, percussive snapping of various bones, including a spine, and as ribcage buckled, everything unattached within that monstrous body was violently expelled. Spurting, spraying fluids in all directions, and, spat out like a constipated man's triumph, the upper half of a body that had once been deeply embedded within a murky, diluvian world. Coughing, hacking, flinging out gobbets of weird phlegm, Birds Mottle reeled away, falling down between hull and splintered gangway.

While the lich raised itself up from the leaking carcass of its foe, fists lifting in exaltation, head rocking back as it prepared to loose a howl of entirely gratuitous glee.

But even the dullest scholar knew that forces in nature were inextricably bound to certain laws. That which plunges downward, in turn launches upward. At least, that which floated on the seas did, just that. Upward, then, the floor, shooting the lich straight up—another such law, one permitting the invention of things as, say, catapults—

And the gnarled, hard-boned, vaguely Ably Drutherly head—for the lich was all too corporeal at the moment—smashed like a battering ram, up through the foredeck's planks. And jammed there.

Momentarily blinded by the concussion, the lich

failed in comprehending the sudden shouts that surrounded it.

"Kick it!"

"Kick it! Kick it!"

All at once, hard-toed boots slammed into the lich's head, from all sides, snapping cheek bones, brow ridges, maxilla, mandible, temporal, frontal. Kick kick kick *slam slam slam*—and then a boot crashed into the lich's gaping, fanged mouth.

And so it bit down.

❭ ❭ ❭

As the horrifying creature bit off half of his right foot, Gust Hubb howled, staggered back, spinning as blood sprayed, and fell to the deck. Toes—now missing—were being ground to meal in the lich's jaws, crusty nails breaking in all the wrong ways, even as more boots hammered at the crumpled, deformed head. Chewing, aye, just like one ear was being chewed, the other gnawed to nearly nothing now and hearing only slow leaking fluids, and as for his nose, well, he was smelling mud. Cold, briny, slimy mud.

Any more of this and he was going to lose his mind.

Someone fell to knees beside him, and he heard

Mipple cry out— "Stick his foot in a bucket!" And then she laughed like the ugly mad woman she was.

↭ ↭ ↭

Snarling (and chewing), the lich retreated from the pummeling, back down through the hole, and as it blinked one of its still functioning eyes, it caught the brief blur that was Birds Mottle—who had, upon retrieving Ably Druther's shortsword—rushed to close, the broad, savage blade plunging deep into the lich's chest.

Shrieking, the creature batted the woman away with a half-dozen arms, sending her flying, skidding and finally tumbling.

Tugging out and flinging aside the offending weapon, the lich advanced on the obnoxious mortal. Paused a moment when something big that had been in its mouth suddenly lodged in its throat. Paused, then, to choke briefly before dislodging the pulpy mass of boot leather, meat, bone, nail and, sad to say, hair. Greater indignity followed, when it shook its head, only to have its lower jaw fall off to thump accusingly pugnacious at its feet.

The roar that erupted from its gaping overbite was more a wheezing gargle, no less frightening as far as Birds Mottle was concerned, for, shrieking, she crabbed back along the gangway, into the grainy patch beneath the hold, then past that, heading for the stern—where, from above and, indeed, from the strongroom behind her, there came sounds of ferocious fighting.

Long-fingered, clawed hands with bits of meat hanging from them lifted threateningly, and the lich stamped ever closer.

ᔍ ᔍ ᔍ

EMANCIPOR REESE'S FRANTIC REACH CAUGHT BENA Younger's skinny ankle, halting her headlong flight towards the giant fiend scrabbling aboard at the stern. The manservant grunted as the girl's weight nearly ripped his arm from its socket, then, as she swung straight down, he heard the thump of her forehead against the mast, the crack of her arms against the top yard—

At that moment, the ship's prow surged back down, whipping the mast and crow's nest hard forward. Something hammered into Emancipor's back and withered, bony arms buffeted about his head. Toppling backward—dragging Bena Younger back up in the process—Emancipor cursed and flung an elbow at the clattering corpse assaulting him. Elbow into shrunken chest, sending the thing flying—and over the edge—

ᕬ ᕬ ᕬ

GUST HUBB ROLLED ONTO HIS BACK, IN TIME TO SEE A ghastly hag plunge down from the night sky, straight at him. Screaming, he threw up his hands just as the thing crashed down onto him.

Knobby, desiccated finger stabbed his left eye and Gust heard a *plop!* as of a crushed grape. Shrieking, he flailed at his attacker. An inward drawn breath netted him a mouthful of brittle, grimy hair.

"Kill it!" someone shouted, voice breaking in hysteria.

"Kill it! Kill it!"

And now boots slammed into Gust, heels cracking down indiscriminately, breaking bones dead and living it was no matter, no matter at all.

"Kill it!"

"It's already dead!"

"Kill it some more!"

Sudden bloom of light as a boot cracked into the side of Gust's misused skull, then darkness.

ᕬ ᕬ ᕬ

IN THE STRONGROOM, OH, IN THE STRONGROOM. AND BACK,

now, a timeward score of rapid steps—

Striding in, Korbal Broach paused to look round, took another stride and saw torn fragments of burlap littering the floor. Behind him, Briv, Briv and Briv edged in, crouched and whispering and at least one of them whimpering.

The Sech'kellyn attacked from all sides. One moment, gloom and calm, the next, explosive mayhem. Stony fists lashed out, sending Brivs flying in all directions. More fists cracked into Korbal Broach, forcing surprised grunts from the huge eunuch. He started punching back. Deathly white bodies reeled, crunched against the curving walls

Briv, Cook's helper, glanced over to see all six of the demons close in on the eunuch. *Just as it should be, him in charge and all that.* Then, spying the motionless, crumpled form of another Briv, he crawled over, grasped the sailor by the ankles, and began dragging Briv—Briv, Rope Braider—away from the colossal battle in the centre of the room.

Briv, Carpenter's helper, was suddenly at Briv's side, taking one of Briv's ankles.

"Hey," Briv, Carpenter's helper, hissed, "Briv's hair got torn off! Hey, this ain't Briv—it's Gorbo!"

"Of course it is!" snapped Briv, Cook's helper. "Everybody knows that!"

"I didn't!"

Cook's helper paused. "That's impossible—you slept with him!"

"Only once! And it was dark—and some women like it—"

"Enough of that, help me get him outa here!"

"What about the wig?"

"What about it?"

"Uh, nothing, I guess."

Hard to tell who was winning—oh, no, easy to tell. Korbal Broach was being beaten to a pulp. Amazing he was still standing, but standing was a good thing, for as long as he stood there the demons weren't bothering with them, and as soon as they got out past the threshold, well, they'd be saved!

⟿ ⟿ ⟿

AS SOON AS THE GOD-THING'S HEAD CLEARED THE RAIL, Bauchelain stepped forward and swung his sword. Edge smashing into the creature's snout. At the blow, something spat out from the mouth.

Line, hook and ear.

A giant taloned hand slashed in a lateral sweep that Bauchelain not quite succeeded in evading, and the curved claws raked slashes through his chain hauberk. Black links pattered like hail across the aft deck.

He chopped down at the limb as it passed, felt the iron bite deep into the wrist, slicing clean through at least one of the bones.

The god wailed.

Bauchelain caught but a glimpse of the other arm, slanting down directly from above, and so he brought up his sword in a blocking parry that was, alas, unsuited to the downward force of the fist's blow, akin to a blacksmith's anvil dropped from a tenement roof.

Blow struck.

Wood crunched, the fist pounding onto the deck, and Bauchelain was no longer on the aft deck.

He landed, amidst showering splinters of wood, in the strongroom.

A Sech'kellyn lunged at him. Instinctively he stop-thrust and watched the demon impale itself on the sword. It cried out, chest shattering like a chunk of marble beneath a mason's spike.

That cry was heard from above. Bellowing, the god began tearing away the aft deck.

The five remaining Sech'kellyn all looked up. Child-like squeals erupted, and all at once the Sech'kellyn was scrabbling up toward the ever-expanding hole. A huge hand reached down and the homunculi climbed it as if scampering up a tree.

A cacophony of screams from just outside the

strongroom door. Rising, a bloodied mass of wounds, Korbal Broach shook himself, glanced once at Bauchelain, then walked out of the strongroom.

ᔧ ᔧ ᔧ

Birds Mottle stared up at the looming lich. She was still trying to scream but her voice was gone, completely gone, and now she was—absurdly—making sounds virtually identical to the lich.

Briv, Briv and Gorbo tumbled into her, the relief on their faces transforming in an instant to mindless terror upon seeing the lich, still looming as dastardly monsters were wont to do.

At that precious moment, with death mimed by every spasmodic clutch of those all-too-many clawed, skeletal hands, with eyes of lifeless black inviting the blackness of lifelessness, with the princely overbite and nasal, wheezing haw-hawing of what was probably intended to be gleeful triumph—at that moment, aye, the lich looked up from its intended victims.

As Korbal Broach strode up to it, stepping right over Birds Mottle's despair-numbed legs, and, smiling, closed his thick-fingered hands to either side of the lich's misshapen head.

A sudden twist to one side, a sharp snap.

Then another sudden twist, to the other side, and grinding sounds.

A twist the other way again, then back again, faster and faster.

With a dry sob the lich's body dropped away beneath the head, clattering onto the gangway in a jumble of limbs, brows, mouths and stuff.

Korbal Broach held the head before him. Still smiling, he turned about.

And looked over to Bauchelain, who appeared in the threshold and was now brushing splinters of wood from his shoulders.

"Look!" piped Korbal Broach.

Bauchelain paused. "I see."

Tucking the mangled head under an arm, Korbal Broach walked to the steps, and up he went.

➳ ➳ ➳

EMANCIPOR REESE LOOKED DOWN ON THE WRECKAGE THAT was the *Suncurl*. Oh, the damned thing still floated, and that was something. The giant reptile thing and its pallid pups were gone, back over the ruined stern, back down into the wretched waters of Laughter's End.

Captain Sater was drunk, leg-sprawled with her back against the prow step, with Cook beside her intoning some discordant declamatory drivel the genius of which was so loftily profound that only he had the wit to comprehend it. Or at least pretend to, which in this world and all others was pretty much the same thing, amen.

He saw Korbal Broach emerge from the hold hatch, something tucked under an arm and guess what that might be—no need, oh no, but guess anyway—and followed a moment later by four sailors all watery with relief and then Bauchelain, who was not quite as solid on his legs as was usual.

To the east, the sky was paling, moments from painting the seas blood-red but too late for that, hey?

A raspy voice cackled behind him, then said, "Mother did what needed doing. We're safe, lass, safe as can be now!"

Emancipor Reese glanced back over a shoulder, then sighed.

Fools.

Groaning, with a last look back at Bena Younger, Emancipor Reese clambered out of the crow's nest and began the climb down.

⇆ ⇆ ⇆

KORBAL BROACH REAPPEARED BRIEFLY ON DECK ONLY TO descend into the hold once more. He emerged a hundred heartbeats later grunting under the weight of a massive, misshapen bladder-like thing replete with limp rat tails and tiny clawed feet all curled in tragic demise. And hundreds of dusty, wrinkled, tiny black eyes none of which took note of the small crowd of staring sailors while Korbal carried it to the foredeck.

Once there he unhitched a grappling hook, checked its knot at both ends, then, crouching down, he impaled the mass of meat on the hook, straightened with a grunt and heaved the mess over the side. A loud splash, then the line paid out for a time.

Standing nearby, quite apart from the crew and their captain who'd watched with mouth hanging open and now a thread of drool dangling, Emancipor Reese frowned at his master at his side. "Uh, fishing with that…."

Bauchelain gave a single nod, then clapped his manservant on the shoulder—making Emancipor wince as a bruise flared beneath that friendly blow—and said, "Think even a dhenrabi, crazed as it might be in this season of mating, would pass up such a sweet morsel, Mister Reese?"

Emancipor shook his head.

Bauchelain smiled down at him. "We shall be towed for a time, yes, to hasten our journey. The sooner we are freed of the lees of Laughter's End, the better, I should think. Do you not agree, Mister Reese?"

"Aye, Master. Only, how do we know where that dhenrabi might take us?"

"Oh, we know that, most certainly. Why, the dhenrabi breeding beds, of course."

"Oh."

"Stay close to the prow, Mister Reese, with knife at the ready."

"Knife?"

"Of course." Another savage clap on the same shoulder. "To cut the rope at the opportune moment."

Emancipor squinted forward, saw the line's sharp downward angle. "How about now, Master?"

"You are being silly, Mister Reese. Now, I think I shall take my breakfast below, assuming Cook is willing."

"Willing? Oh, aye, Master, he is that I'm sure."

"Excellent."

⌒ ⌒ ⌒

GUST HUBB OPENED HIS REMAINING EYE AND FOUND himself staring up at Heck Urse's face.

That now smiled. "Ah, awake now, are ya? Good. Here, let me help you sit up a bit. You lost more than a bucket full of blood, you need your food and Cook's gone and made up some gruel just for you, friend. No ears, no nose, half a foot and broke bones, you're a mess."

"Bucket?"

"Oh, aye, Gust, more than a bucket full—I saw the bucket, I did."

Heck Urse then spooned some slop into Gust Hubb's mouth.

He choked, fought back a gag reflex, swallowed, then swallowed some more, finally coming up for a gasp of air.

Heck Urse nodded. "Better?"

"Aye. Cook's a poet, Heck, a real poet."

"That he is, friend. That he is."

⮜ ⮜ ⮜

DISPERSED, NAY FLUNG AWAY LIKE SO MUCH DROSS, SOULS found themselves once more trapped within iron nails embedded in wood.

"I told you a mercantile venture would've been better," Master Baltro said.

"I'm not ready for oblivion, oh no," hissed Viviset. "Once I escape—"

"You won't escape," cut in the one voice (apart from the Jhorligg's and they'd heard just about enough from it, thank you very much) that didn't belong to any nail. "Dead currents are cutting into the Red Road now. Our chance is lost, forever lost."

"Who in Hood's name are you, anyway?" demanded Hag Threedbore.

"I wish I knew."

"Well, go away," said Threedbore, "we don't like your kind around here."

"A mercantile venture—"

"Something's nibbling my spleen!" cried Lordson Hoom.

⌒ ⌒ ⌒

THROUGH THE SCARRED CRYSTAL LENS, THE *SUNCURL* wallowed fitful and forlorn, and the huge man standing at the prow of *Unreasoning Vengeance* slowly lowered the eyepiece. He turned about and studied his eleven brothers and two sisters, not one short or even of average height, not one not bound in massive muscle—women included—and he smiled.

"Blessed kin, we have them."

All fourteen now set to preparing their weapons. Two-handed axes, two-handed swords (one of them a three-hander thanks to an overly ambitious but not too intelligent weapon smith back in Toll's City), falchions, mattocks, mauls, maces, flails, halberds and one very nasty looking stick. Armour glinted as it was wont to do in morning sunlight; helms were donned, indeed, jammed down hard over thick-boned skulls. Silver-sheathed tusks gleamed on a few of the men who betrayed more than the normal hints of Jagh blood.

Around them swarmed the crew, all undead since that saved feeding and watering them and they never slept besides, while down below in the hold enormous, starving beasts growled and roared in frenzied hunger, pounding against their cages.

Tiny Chanter, the eldest in the family and so its leader, unslung his own weapon, a two-ended thing with one end a crescent-bladed axe and spike and the other a studded mace that had the word SATRE painted on it in red, because Tiny couldn't spell, and then scanned his kin once more.

"We have them," he repeated.

And he smiled again.

All the Chanters smiled.

One undead sailor, noting this, screamed.